Gatherings Volume XII

The En'owkin Journal of
First North American Peoples

Transformation

Fall 2001

edited by Florene Belmore
& Eric Ostrowidzki

Theytus Books Ltd.
Penticton, BC

Gatherings
The En'owkin Journal of First North American Peoples Volume XII
2001

Copyright © 2001 for the authors

National Library of Canada Cataloguing in Publication Data
Main entry under title:

Gatherings

Annual.
ISSN 1180-0666   ISBN 1-894778-00-6
1. Canadian literature (English)--Indian authors--Periodicals.* 2. Canadian literature (English)--Periodicals.* 3. American literature--Indian authors--Periodicals. 4. American literature--Periodicals. I. En'owkin International School of Writing. II. En'owkin Centre.
PS8235.I6G35 C810.8'0897   CS91-0314837
PR9194.5.I5G35

Editorial Committee: Florene Belmore, Eric Ostrowidzki and Greg Young-Ing
Cover Art: Debby Keeper
Design: Florene Belmore
Typesetting/Proofing: Chick Gabriel, Leanne Flett Kruger and Audrey Huntley

Please send submissions and letters to *Gatherings*, En'owkin Centre, R.R. 2, Site 50, Comp.8 Penticton, BC, V2A 6J7, Canada. Previously published works are not considered.

The publisher acknowledges the support of the Canada Council for the Arts, the Department of Canadian Heritage and the British Columbia Arts Council in the publication of this book.

Table of Contents

Florene Belmore	Editor's Note/7
Eric Ostrowidzki	Editor's Note/9

SECTION 1 – Naked Truth

Annie Rose Major	Naked Truth/13
	A Little Cube/15
Cathy Ruiz	Passion/16
	In Winnipeg/18
	Those Letters/20
Janet Rogers	Warrior Reflection/22
Amy-Jo Setka	Tilt/24
D.D. Moses	Flaming Nativity/26
Mary Caesar	A Dedication/31
	School of Horrors/32
	Hands of Rage and Wrath/33
Mariel Belanger	Always and Forever/35
	As the Days Pass/36
	My Brother and Me/36
	White Wolf/37
Barbara Vibbert	Left Behind/38
	The Crows/39
Karen Olson	The Red Top/41
Heather Harris	Coyote and the Anthropologist/48
	The Question of Cousins/50

SECTION 2 – Reflection

Debby Keeper	See/55
	I want to feel... /56
	i am/57

Table of Contents

Jack D. Forbes	In the Dunes/58
	Suspended Animation/66
	Getaway/70
Charles L. Mack	Repo Cowboys... /79
Candy Zazulak	Frogman/86
Sandra A. Olsen	Across Many Miles/87
Connie Crop Eared Wolf	My Friend Tamra/90
Theresa G. Norris	Maria/91
Brent Peacock	Frustration/97
William George	Squamish Floods/99
	They Rose And So Shall I/101
MariJo Moore	Atop Palacca on First Mesa/102
Bernelda Wheeler	Education is Our Buffalo/111
	The Souls Inside of Them/114

SECTION 3 – Metamorphosis

Bernelda Wheeler	Requiem for a Country Daughter/119
Bradlee LaRocque	Failing Peyote 101/121
Duane Niatum	The Story of Our Name/122
Karen Olson	Blood of the Earth/127
Margaret McKay-Sinclair Ruiz	My Memoirs/134
Janet Duncan	unchartered territory/137
Donald Blais	Timely License Deliberately Circumnavigated/140
Karen Coody Cooper	As The Prow Cuts Through Water/143

Table of Contents

Fran Pawis	For the Children/145
	Inspiration Encourages Transformation/146
	Soon/147
April Severin	Testimony/149
Shirley Brozzo	My People Paid/150
	Misshepeshu/152
Gordon de Frane	Oldest Medicine in the World/154
Eric Ostrowidzki	Yo, Brown Skinned Girls... /161
Richard Van Camp	Twenty Music Videos... /168
	I Go Bazook!/172

SECTION 4 – Redemption

Kimberly TallBear	A Nomad's Sleep/175
	Strange Gift/176
	Between Nations/179
	Anonymity/180
Rasunah Marsden	Refuge/181
R. Vincent Harris	Souls, Fire, Air, Water, Feathers/186
Janet Rogers	Life Beat/190
Jerry L. Gidner	Flute/192
Mary Caesar	Northern Sky Dancers/194
Sherri L. Mitchel	Sky Woman/195
Amy-Jo Setka	Tea Ceremony/196
Allison Hedge Coke	Memoir Excerpt – Fish/198
Tracey Kim Jack	Stars for Mary/201
Theresa G. Norris	David the Bear/204

Table of Contents

Carolyn Kenny	The Dream and the Vision/208
Linda LeGarde Grover	*Migwechiwendam* (English)/213 *Migwechiwen*/214 Redemption/215

SECTION 5 – Horizons: Voices of Our Youth

Joleen Terbasket	Canoe Trip/221
Joseph Louis	Caged/222
Johnny Lee Bonneau	Relate/223
Rachel Bach and Leah Morgan	Star Gars/224
Shawn Wildcat	Untitled/229
Shannon Wildcat	Generations/230 Looking Back/231

Biographies/233

Editor's Note

We are once again proud to present another annual volume of of *Gatherings: The En'owkin Journal of First North American Peoples*. The theme of Volume XII is "Transformation" and the work by Indigenous authors in the sections within will take you through personal journeys of realization, reflection, change and coming to terms with new realities.

As the Western World bows its head in an uneasy fear that the global order is forever transformed, we sympathize with the memory of the many massacres and acts of violence that have been inflicted upon Indigenous Peoples in various parts of the world, including Canada, the United States, Mexico, Guatemala, Chile, New Caledonia, East Timor, Rawanda and Tibet. The tenacity of Indigenous Peoples is testimony that nations under threat can reach down deep and endure through difficult times ensuring their protection and survival.

Through the metamorphosis from colonization to de-colonization, Indigenous Peoples have also gone through great individual transformations many of which you will read about in the following pages. As with each new volume of *Gatherings*, a wide range of genres and perspectives are featured and it is always a pleasure to publish this collection of fresh and vibrant Indigenous voices.

In Strength,
Florene Belmore

Editor's Note

Asked to write about how I felt reading these writers as I worked on *Gatherings XII*, I first noticed that there were similarities in the writing. There are voices coming from the same place of crouching darkness or smooth soaring curve of blue sky; common spools of ideas; and the deep-textured whorl of lived lives.

Convergent histories – radiating and scintillating and dimming like a holographic medallion whose shifting image is too bright or too vast to behold.

With each black lettered page, I began to hear that these writers have all come from different regions, have had different experiences of grit, laughter and beauty, have different ways of the lean and arch of the body and the tilt of the face towards the sun. And then I began to detect within these many voices – within those rustling currents of live speech – the differences in diction and meanings and stories, of rhythms jotted or typed in the murmuring codes of blood. The ineffable power of their language and talent, bellowing or singing!

Yet despite the similarities or differences or the accuracy or inaccuracy of my own observations, there was an image that lingered on in my mind long after reading these pieces. Aided by graphic signs on these pages, I imagined millions of signal fires burning hotly and greenly across these Indigenous nations – not like the light-board of a "Sprint Telemarketing Map" – but fires communicating in emerald tongues with each other far into deepest night and across the plains of tomorrow.

All My Relations,
Eric Ostrowidzki

Naked Truth

Annie Rose Major

Naked Truth

Naked truth, intense, lying there with open arms,
All feeling gone, silence in death,
Revealing itself as dawn awakens,
Not a breath to tell

Naked truth, who knows, only the night holds its secret,
A whisper here a whisper there reveals its ingredient,
Silent as a panther,
Stalking its prey with death in its paws

Naked truth, a victim stands alone in a darkened street,
Inviting its enemy, caught unaware,
Wearing its addiction like a crown

Naked truth, steadily the enemy approaches,
Leading its victim now
Above the darkened street
To its hellish haven

Naked truth, silence as dead as the night,
Echoes of days gone by,
It feeds its disgusting thirst

Naked truth with its tainted black liquid
And stiff pressed suits,
It lures its prey
And strikes its deathly blow

Naked truth with a drive so intense
It strikes again and again,
Never giving an edge,
Only to its black liquid

Annie Rose Major

Naked truth has reached its climax,
Slipping beneath the carpeted hallways,
Smelling its deathly smell

Naked truth slipping out into society,
Pains echoes out into the night,
The panther has been discovered

Naked truth, it's shackled now,
This tainted liquid
Placed upon its heathen throne,
Bowing now to hide its guilt

Naked truth, its tainted soul has been released
Out into society where it began its reign,
Roaming free... to strike again.

Annie Rose Major

A Little Cube

A little here,
A little there,
A nibble here,
A chew there,
A little cube,
I did bite,
Now I shiver,
Into the night,

A little shiver,
A little shake,
A quiver here,
A tremble there,
A little cube
I did bite,
Now I shiver,
Into the night.

Cathy Ruiz

Passion

For Michelle. BC, Canada - 1995

She took two fillet knives,
walked into the bathroom
folded herself, tall, slender into the tub
then sank the blades, once, twice, three times, into
her chest.

I, far away, took my third bite of Chinese food
watching my former lover's eyes, his lips
remember how lightening
and thunder sliced the skies
while we lay entangled under trees.

As life flowed from her pale body, inching over
enamel and into the drain, the bathroom light
grew smaller and smaller in her eyes,
while smoke curled from his cigarette to the ceiling
above the table where I sat.

Her father bent over her, suffering
the limp heart that had never known
a man's love, carried away on a stretcher
while I dismissed myself from the table, seeing again
in his smile how he played women like dice,
but wouldn't I still love to kiss him.

As she lay prone on a morgue bed,
brown eyes, stilled spirit staring,
I slept fitfully with the past, the future,
until the telephone drew my mother's voice,
into my ear, "Michelle killed herself last night."

Cathy Ruiz

"She took two fillet knives,
walked into the bathroom
folded herself, tall, slender into the tub
then sank the blades, once, twice, three times, into
her chest."
I saw her wounded, 23-year-old body,
her life, now a breath running past me.
So passionate, I thought, before whispering,
"Good bye."

Cathy Ruiz

In Winnipeg

Shrouded in darkness,
a Manitoba town hung suspended, captured
in a haze of thirty-seven below.
In Winnipeg,
a frozen wasteland awaited
to pack me in its cold storage.
Muffled city,
lost in a maze of six-foot snow drifts,
still welcomed a Metis daughter.

Hotel lobby,
heated cabin at the end of an airport trapline,
was a sacred place for loons and geese,
calling out from marshes and lakes
in the red, black, yellow, and blues
of traditional Native painting.
Tall, black-haired Metis businessmen,
grinning shyly, slapped black buckskin muckluks and
gloves,
bright beads, white fur trim gleaming
on the hotel desk,
their sweet whisperings
clicked with Cree tongues rode with me
up to the 22nd
floor.

My thoughts,
my heart, beat along with Native drumming
in nearby rooms,
while through ice-framed windows puffs of steam rose
like ghosts spreading ethereal fingers toward the sky.
My hopes sang
for the northern lights-the spirits of Elders come

back to earth
to dance one last time with the rest of the tribe.
"The swish you hear
is the movement of their dress," my mother's voice
reminded
in the silence.
At midnight,
a wailing train across the Assiniboine River
told me to abandon my post
while the full moon, riding high above the city,
taunted, "Crawl under the covers and hibernate!"

Cathy Ruiz

Those Letters

I burned those letters
that I'd kept locked in a heavy black chest
that always took two to move. I'd hung onto those words
for too long.
Too long I'd treated those letters like they were
precious weapons,
carved my needs with their words; included their final ritual
in my will.

Did they speak of love?
Perhaps.
But I treated them as though they held the only secret
of my life
in love.

Well, I finally let go of all that. I tossed those
letters into a box,
then, out the door, into a wheelbarrow
and across the yard they went.
Landed right on top of a big bonfire of brush and
brambles.
Clearing land you know.
I had to.

I stood there and watched as those old words
that once kept my heart cold–loss can be like
that–turn brown,
the pages curl
and the lines of ink smear
into char,
until those letters became a fine, black tissue,

Cathy Ruiz

bits of which whirled up and over the treetops
and I, down below,
my heart beat warm
in my chest.

Janet Rogers

Warrior Reflection

Walking down the street, I passed a store window that had an attractive red shirt I thought I would like to buy
then I realized it was the Eddie Bauer store.

WHAT IS HAPPENING TO ME?

Last week, a gang of boys passed my house, making noise, rough-housing. They looked to be 14 or 15 years old. As I watched them pass from the safety of my own home, I picked out 1 or 2 of them I wouldn't mind doing.

WHAT IS HAPPENING TO ME?

I noticed lately, I drive my car everywhere. To friends, to work, to the post office, to the Chinese food place around the corner from me. And as I rolled into a parkade downtown where the rate was $2.50 per hour, I remember thinking, that's a fair price.

WHAT IS HAPPENING TO ME?

I almost watched a Barbara Streisand movie the other day.

WHAT IS HAPPENING TO ME?

I went on a trip, met a guy, we had an affair and when I left he invited me to visit him in his town. I actually thought he was serious there for a second.

WHAT IS HAPPENING TO ME?

The grey hair is coming in all over, the skin is becoming loose. My taste for candy and crisps is still intact, but my stomache wages war afterward.

Janet Rogers

I am up early, and in bed just after sunset.
You know, I've even taken an interest in sewing lately

WHAT THE HELL IS HAPPENING TO ME?

My spirit used to be reckless and winning, proud and stinging.
Now it bows to prudence and patience, wisdom and willingness.
What has tamed my penchant for danger?
And what fields is the Red Warrior in me now riding through?
Has she forsaken me at the cost of a steady pay cheque?
Will I meet her again somewhere down the road?

Upon our meeting, she may well ask,

WHAT HAPPENED TO YOU?

Amy-Jo Setka

Tilt

1

Been thinking, ranting in my head
Can this panicky feeling be helped?
The invisible hand is crushing us
money media manifest destiny
O no O no the WTO
Gas masks illegal
Prices soaring for products to further pollute the planet
voices drowned in pepper, batons, boots and bullets
rubber or not they are shooting the people
Acts committed daily in white supremacist society
destroy dignity Evil Pain Injustice Lies
Conspiratorial Industrial Military web
Corporate control of Neo-colonial domination
Who holds the patent on your stem cells?
This battle began long ago
everyday the casualties pile up as they
report the losses in blase bourgeois voices
We swear we can smell the bodies
How can the people win without playing their game?
Are we conscious or critical
Cargill Kraft Dupont General Electric Coca fucking Cola Mcmurder the Mcmasses
Economic reality built on brutality and the lie of never ending growth

2

Our money goes to Feed the soldiers Buy the bullets Slaughter the trees
Can't read the newspapers, we've used all our tears
The invisible hand is killing us
We must find our footing face the monster face first with hearts full
so we can begin
We have to do this right and now
Together. We have been divided for so long, How do you think we lost control?

Amy-Jo Setka

A moment of clarity where we can see beyond
There are ways to live in this world with grace
lightness and trust in the gift of all that is or ever will be
This is a place of infinite possibilities. Amen.

Daniel David Moses

Flaming Nativity
about Billy Merasty's 'Fireweed'

So have you heard the one about the faggot Indian?

Maybe I should have said "the Indian faggot."

Oh, whichever epithet I might choose to use hardly makes much difference. Your answer is most likely "No." Hey, why use two, both sticks and stones, why overdo it, when either one would be sufficient to the put down? Yeah, either one has always been enough to build a good story around.

Until now, of course, when some of them Indians have begun to ram this damn political – or is it historical or cultural? – correctness down our throats.

Why can't they take a joke? Hell, talk about doing Kawlija.

First Nations? Just what is the story there? It sounds like a brand of diapers. Native renaissance, my ass. On second thought, never mind my ass.

"Hey, have you heard the one about the First Nation faggot?" just doesn't work. Oh joke, where is thy sting?

And – wouldn't you know it? – now they're starting to reassert stories about their national identities. It was so much simpler when they all were just Indians. Hey, you can't live in the past. We're supposed to be able to tell that there's something different between that Cree and this Delaware or whatever? Aren't we all just Canadians?

Who's doing the coyote calls?

And now that they're rediscovering their traditional cultures, some of them are actually trying to do away with that old and trusty set of insults, faggot, fairy, queer, sissy – even the kids can use them! – and replace them with this New Agey sounding 'two-spirit' thing. I mean, talk about limp wristed. Aren't Indians supposed to be warriors? Real men? That's the story I'm used to hearing.

And what about their morals? They do not to seem to give an American plug nickel that the Judeo-Christian God might not like this threat to the fertility of the tribe. Yeah, strangely enough, it seems like their *Gitchy Manitou*, their Great Mystery, actually made some people queer so they could serve, in the interest of harmony, as intermediaries between the divisions of the world, women and men, life and death – us and Ottawa maybe.

What next? Jesus and all the apostles notwithstanding, if this keeps up, 'gay' is going to start sounding really normal. Oh for the days of yore when it was just something Christmasy, whenever that was...

"Have you heard the one about the two-spirited Cree?" just isn't funny.

So what about this 'Fireweed' play by William (Billy) Merasty? What about its cutely ironic subtitle 'An Indigeni Fairy Tale' ?

Well, okay, okay, if we are to believe what it says, maybe I should have said "Have you heard the one about the two-spirited Cree? It isn't *just* funny." It's also glamourous in the original sense, charming our imaginations with actual magic tricks as well as a full hand of more usual theatrics – fire, light and lightning, sound, character, stories and their telling.

Its central story of a journey toward healing and home is also a story about escaping that dark side of glamour, the curse, which is laid down in this particular plot by, of course, a man in black, a priest. We would be offended by this pitiful church bashing if we were not also being teased by this twist on the usual fairy tale, this seemingly new or at least naughty and possibly even feminist (Who knew Native culture would have to do with women too?) point of view – although if we are to trust the teller, it is an ancient way of seeing. No wonder, despite all the anguish of the story's journey, it remains seductive, mysterious, erotic.

Which is of course why, though 'Fireweed' may be the first one we here have heard tell of these doubly epitheted individuals, faggot Indians, Indian faggots, it is certainly not going to be the last. Who knew we could get into such bent and effeminate territory by following this Native renaissance movement? Who knew a Native nativity might involve more than feathered headdresses and war paint, and how, yes, how the Hiawatha did they keep quiet about it for so long?

How the heart of Merasty's 'Fireweed' aches for lost loves, for suicides and those who are taught by the church to hate themselves, the queers and the Indians. But then it remembers how heart beats go on.

Its central character Peechweechum Rainbowshield, referred to hereafter as Rainbow, thrown into a holding cell in nothing but his underwear, insulted and assaulted by a police officer, somehow pulls a little red dress, lip stick and high heels out of nowhere. The beautiful young man proceeds to do a drag musical number as his version of the great escape act, disappearing, the vanishing Indian, from that Winnipeg jail into the dream stream of the play.

He slips through the iron bars and stones of the white man's law and religion and right into his and our community's mythology much the same way his predecessor, the legendary medicine dreamer, Isiah Iskootee'oo, did in the long ago to the frustration of the Royal Canadian Mounted Police. Isiah Iskootee'oo escaped punishment, the story goes, for setting fire to the bush, destroying Her Majesty's timber. But now that we have recovered the knowledge – the Native renaissance again – that burning was used traditionally to manage forest environments and facilitate hunting, Isiah Iskootee'oo's misdemeanor appears in a more heroic light.

So the scene in 'Fireweed' where Rainbow escapes, theatrically, magically, perhaps – yes – perhaps incredibly (it is early in the renaissance after all), from laws that would punish him for a crime called 'Gross Indecency' may just be a first and teasing glimpse of recovered knowledge, an alternative mythology, and some common sense about sexual behavior.

The scene is certainly pivotal to the play, erupting spontaneous theatrical combustion, burning down the fourth wall. The character Rainbow is allowed to step out of the narrative, as well as his cell, and play with and to us in the audience, just like the characters of the Flight Attendant or Reena Lightningway or even the Judge who are all spirits and not limited by flesh and blood bodies or dramaturgical realities.

'Fireweed' before this scene is a story about Rainbow, a young man haunted and made almost hopeless by the suicide of his beloved twin brother in the inferno of a burning church. He is haunted by the possibility that he, a medicine minded young Cree, as the object not only of his rather Catholic brother's love but of his sexual desire, may have been the cause of a great sin – is the dilemma faith or homosexuality or incest or all the above? He fears he may have been the cause of his brother's suicide.

This spiritual murkiness is lit only by the presence of the above mentioned guardian spirits (the 'fairy god parents' the play's ironic subtitle invokes) and the Manitoba Legislature's Golden Boy, emblem here of the possibility of love. The play suggests a version of Winnipeg that is a sort of hell on earth, streets where sex, drugs, and rock and roll are never expressions of growth, exploration, joy and youth, but always mean meaningless, directionless despair.

Rainbow's little red dress number redresses this. After its performance, like magic, the story, the stories 'Fireweed' tells take on a motive, become hopeful, helpful, loving, and shift Rainbow toward reconciliation with his two-spirited self and his family (his most Catholic mother) and his community (his auntish medicine teacher). He is saved at the same time his former lover Raven is lost. It may be that because Rainbow is able to accept and express, even so campily, his own female spirit that he finds his way home.

Rainbow's little red dress number acts like a front door into a strangely familiar house, a dream world, a memory of adolescence when the erotic was more than the body, was what the whole world was about. The drag number is itself the essence of queer, two-spirited, both true and false, male and female, and is the play's intermediary between us (the audience) and them, our forgotten desires, our bodies.

The home Rainbow returns to is a place not only of pristine wilderness but also of ancient stories, a mythology that is a way to wisdom about our lives, about the body and its hungers. No wonder Rainbow needs to hear again the ones about Weesageechak, the Cree trickster, needs to relive one of that great spirit's adventures.

The Weetigo, that embodiment of morbid hunger, traps and threatens to eat Weesageechak, much as western civilization does with Indians. Only Weesageechak's own cunning and the help of a weasel who is willing to journey into the Weetigo's body, via its anus and inners, allows Weesageechak to survive --and the weasel to be beautiful. What more visceral, funny, and queer representation of a journey into and through our fears or lives could we ask for?

Hey, shit happens.

Have you heard the one about the Indian faggot and Weesageechak and the Weetigo? Yeah. It proves things have a way of working out in the end.

A Dedication

This is a dedication for the residential school
survivors who have passed on.
There were so many.
They will not be forgotten.
They have suffered but did not survive
to tell their stories.
But we know that their suffering and pain
were not in vain.
That their lives were not wasted.
They were our brave, silent warriors.
Their lives of hardship and suffering
were the evidence and testimonies of their
experiences in the residential school system.
Their memories will forever be carried
and cherished in our hearts and honoured
and revered in our history.

Mary Caesar

School of Horrors

I was eager to go to that mysterious school that my sisters went to.
My sisters would arrive home from the holidays looking scrubbed, groomed and educated.
I was excited about going to that mythical school.
I would daydream and anticipate the day I would board the vehicle that would bring me there.
I did not know where this elusive school was.
I only knew that I was a very inquisitive and curious child.
I wanted to go to that intriguing school that my sisters attended.
In reality, it was fifteen miles south of my hometown.
I wanted to learn to read and write.
I later learned I had no choice in the matter.
My parents would have been jailed if they did not send us children there.
My sisters would bring home books, scribblers and toys, but they came back traumatized.
I sensed it in their quietness.
They weren't the same.
They became subdued.
Later on in my childhood years, I brought home my scribblers, books and dolls.
I learned to be prim and proper but I was becoming rebellious in a quiet, seething way.
The day I was rounded up to begin my education at the school was a sad, emotional day.
I felt sad because my Mom and Dad didn't come with me.
When I arrived at the school, I immediately felt abandoned and rejected.
I stepped off the vehicle, walked up the steps of the school and looked up at the monstrous monolithic building before me.
The school was surrounded by a forest that was my sanctuary for the next four years I was imprisoned there.
It would be the beginning of my introduction to the school of horrors, that would forever change every aspect of my life.

Mary Caesar

Hands of Rage and Wrath

I still feel the sting of her hands
on my face as she struck me.
See her raising her hands,
wagging her stiff forefinger to me
in accusation.
Hear the echo of her voice
as she raised her voice to a shrill whine,
scolding me with her index finger.
She'd close her hands in a fist
and move her index finger in a fast
jerking motion like a moment captured
in a cubist-futurist painting.
She reminded me of an army sergeant
from the Gestapo.
Her favourite expression was, "You mark my words,
Lady Jane, just wait 'til I get my hands on you,
I'll box your ears! Maybe then, you'll pay attention!"
She'd cuff me on different areas of my head,
whenever and wherever she'd find it convenient
to satisfy her warped sense of self-righteous
and sadistic hunger.
She'd appear out of nowhere, out of the blue,
unannounced, unwelcomed.
She'd appear like a fierce tornado to interrupt
our childhood moments of camaraderie,
in the hallways, in the dorms, in the recreation rooms,
to unleash her hatred, her contempt and wickedness.
She caught us off guard when we were not aware of her.
Everyday she'd find excuses to punish us
to satisfy her atrocious actions.
She'd say with disdain, "I'll box your ears!"
Her words dripped with hate as she slurred her favourite expression,
many times during the years I was confined at the school.

Mary Caesar

She'd shape her hands like a bowl and cuff my ears
and on the sides of my head.
I saw her "box" a lot of the girls heads during my four year
confinement.

Mariel Belanger

Always and Forever

I need time to be
Alone
To grieve, to heal
To forget all the pain
And remember the fun
We once had

I'll miss you
I know I've never
Said this to you,
Thinking you would
Always be here
But
I love you brother
Always and forever

Mariel Belanger

As the days pass

As the days pass by
We often sit and wonder why
God chose you to walk alone
The path from life to the unknown

Perhaps your time was through
And that is why he chose you

Your stay with us was brief
But even five years doesn't diffuse the grief
Although your passing was so hard
We know above us you'll stand guard

For one of these days we anticipate
United again will be our fate.

My brother and me

I've heard what Coyote has to say
He deceives me with his trickery
He says, "Come with me and I'll
Show you the way"
He's been to see you and
Knows where you stay

I fight him back, knowing what's true
Creator found better things for you
Still Coyote calls with howls to the moon
"You can't see him but I will soon"
I cry to Creator, "Show me the way"
He tells me, "Be patient there will come a day"
And for this day I anxiously wait
My brother and me in destiny's fate.

Mariel Belanger

White Wolf

White wolf crying
In the middle of the night

Is he calling me this time?
Is he calling me?

White wolf crying
Searching for the one

Will it be me this time?
Will it be me?

White wolf finds me
And shakes his head no

He doesn't want me
It's not my turn

White wolf, I ask
What have you done with my brother?

White wolf cries
I have found him a better place

These poems are dedicated to my brother Marcel Louis Philippe Ducan (J.R.) Belanger, May 21, 1978 to November 15, 1995.

Barbara Vibbert

Left Behind

Left behind
memories of a
mother's breast
rocky crests
all the rest -
Odawa ways.

Left behind
isolation of
new ways learned
stomach churned
small eyes burned
under alien roof.

Left behind
devastation of
sisters dead
future dread
as she said
I will move on.

Left behind
memories of a
life lived bold
time grown old
embers cold
she's laid to rest.

Barbara Vibbert

The Crows

The Crows, the Crows
Came winging in
On scudding skies
And howling winds

Cawing, cawing
From western shore
By twos and threes
They came, still more

Frantic, frantic
Gathering now
On cedar tree
On every bough

Chatter, chatter
Loud and raucous
They gathered there
As if to caucus

Hundreds, hundreds
Loud and boisterous
Flapping feathers
Strident voices

Blackened branches
Limbs aquiver
They rose as one
Raven shimmer

Flying, flying
Hither and yon
No more, no more
The crows are gone!

Barbara Vibbert

Shimmer, shimmer
Through rays of sun
A rainbow frames
The tree. Storm's done.

The Red Top

Sandra Roan looked toward the doorway of the crumbling apartment building trying to remember if she'd ever enjoyed living there. The door was new; dark wood with brass fixtures that gleamed in the pale twilight.

"Of course, it's the only way," she said.

Two days later, a brilliant sunset faded to lush lavender as she turned into the parking lot of Buffalo Skull Lodge. Sandra could see the dark hulk of War Mountain in the distance. The tiny Vega shimmied over to a battered blue truck with a white eagle feather sticker peeling off the driver's window. A real eagle feather hung on a red ribbon from the rearview mirror. The car door creaked open. Cool evening air scented with wood smoke assailed her.

Sandra looked at the mountain. Most of one side was carved off; a jagged treeline neared the middle, but mere root and trunk were no match for solid rock and the trees petered out. She turned when the door to the bar opened; country music blared, the smell of stale beer and smoke reached her. A man wearing a denim shirt with embroidered blue horses on the sleeves and faded jeans stood in the doorway. She didn't know him until the crooked smile.

"Don!" she exclaimed.

Her brother covered the ground in three strides, then wrapped Sandra in his arms.

"It's been too long," she murmured.

Sandra stepped back. She wasn't surprised that she hadn't know him. He'd grown at least two feet.

"Look at you. You must be tall as Dad," she said cheerily.

Don snaked an arm around her waist. "Not quite. He has an inch over me. But you, you haven't changed at all. You're still beautiful. Are you as bossy as ever?"

Sandra laughed, "Remember when I used to make you wear just one leg of your pajamas. You'd shuffle along with both feet sticking out. You looked so funny."

Don shook his head saying, "What about when you used to make me eat lemons? You told me they were sour oranges."

Sandra chuckled as he continued, "Funny thing is, I like lemons now. People around here eat 'em with salt."

They were at the door when Sandra suddenly stopped. She didn't like being around drunks. Since being groped by a group of drunken boys one night during college, she'd avoided bars. Instead, she went to movies or took art lessons. That's how she met Carter Mason; at an oil painting class.

"I thought we could just meet Dad for coffee," Sandra said hesitantly.

Don tilted his head. "There's just a few regulars in there. Don't worry, they're harmless," he said with another lopsided grin.

"I don't go to bars," said Sandra.

Don pulled the door open. A whiskey-voiced woman was singing about lost love on a highway to nowhere. Wisps of smoke glided out the open door. Sandra took a step backward but Don's hand on her back gently pushed her inside.

"C'mon. You'll be okay. It's where Dad always hangs out anyway. Might as well get to know it," he said.

Three old men sitting nearby looked at them. Sandra saw a man try to stand up but he couldn't quite make it and fell back into his seat. His companions laughed. One of them pushed a bottle of beer over which the man took and drank. Sandra turned away, but Don was over at the bar talking to the big woman behind the counter. She looked around.

There must have been a hundred tables inside the bar. Five pool tables on the far side had a few young men and women playing at one. A row of beer glasses was on the ledge behind them. A couple sat at a table near the dance floor; the woman was passed out. Sandra watched her lean to the left, perch there momentarily then slowly move to the right.

"You wanna go?" Don said.

"Sure. I feel really out of place," she said.

Her brother shook his head. "No. I mean do you wanna go see Dad?"

"He's here. Where?"

Don led her toward the table with the old men. Smoke rose in great plumes from the forgotten cigarettes smoldering in the ashtray. She recognized none of them.

"Who is he? Which one?" she whispered fiercely.

The sad love song ended as they reached the table.

"Dad. Sandra's come for a visit," Don said loudly.

A man in a dirty tan jacket stood shakily: it was the same one who'd tried earlier. Six years had changed him. Grey, tangled hair jutted crazily around a slack face marred with red spidery lines across the nose and cheeks. The cracked lips smiled showing a few stained teeth. Finally, Sandra recognized the eyes. They were as black and fierce as ever.

One of the men slapped him on the back saying, "Say something Donny Boy. It's yer girl come back."

"Yeah. By God, it's my little Sandy," he mumbled.

Sandra was repulsed. Her father lunged toward her. She staggered under the weight, almost gagging at the odor of urine and shit. He began speaking in Blackfoot which made his companions nod and smile. The thin one with two skinny grey braids leaned backwards, staring.

He slurred, "Sure is a pretty little thing. Takes after your side Don. Pretty like your old ma, init?"

The other man smiled, his fat face resembling a Buddha statue in she and Carter's favorite antique store. Sandra smiled weakly at them then gently pushed her father away.

"Can we go somewhere, Dad? To talk?" she asked quietly.

Her father sat, taking up a cigarette with a shaking hand. He inhaled and swung his head back and forth. Sandra felt as though she'd been punched in the stomach, but Don's hand on her arm steadied her. He spoke a few Blackfoot words which seemed to please their father who smiled and jerked his head in agreement.

"Gert's gonna phone when he's ready to come home," said Don, gesturing to the woman he'd been talking to.

Without another word they left. The air felt cool on her flushed face. Sandra took several deep breaths. Twinkling lights from a towering sign turned her bare arms blue. Traffic roared in the background. Sandra wanted to get back on the highway to her life in Calgary. Don's voice stopped her.

"Feel like leaving don't you?"

Sandra lowered her eyes and nodded wearily.

"Yeah. Sometimes I feel like that too. But Dad's not always like this. He goes on a binge, then straightens out for a few weeks. It's almost like he's the old man again," he said.

"Why didn't you tell me he was in such bad shape?" she asked suddenly.

Her brother shook his head saying, "He isn't. At least I know where he is. Bad shape is finding him passed out on the street in the middle of winter or in the hospital after being run over 'cause he stumbled into the road."

She'd come to apologize for her behavior in The Red Top so long ago, and was hoping to be forgiven. Now, the brilliant plan to try rid herself of guilt was in jeopardy. Her father needed help more than she needed his forgiveness.

"Every time we talked you never mentioned anything about...about this," said Sandra gesturing toward the bar.

Her brother put his hands on her shoulders. "Every time? Sandy, other than your call last night we've had three conversations in six years," he said.

Three times. How could that be? Was it true? Sandra thought hard and realized that it was. Her face flamed.

"It's like I almost forget about the two of you. I'm sorry Don," said Sandra.

Her brother bent his knees and looked in her eyes.

"Why did you come?" he asked.

Sandra felt her body sag but Don reached out to hold her

up. Behind him, the dark shape of War Mountain stood like a silent giant. Sandra could feel his hands on her arms shake. When he was little, Don's hands would flutter when he was upset, the fingers moving like he was playing a piano. Sandra almost smiled at the memory.

"Dad's way of coping with Mom's death was to drink himself into oblivion each night. Do you remember how he used to talk about all the good times the family supposedly had?" she said.

It was Don's turn to blush. He'd always agreed with Dad whenever he told a story about events that never happened. But he had wanted to believe those stories. Sandra knew he didn't want to remember what really happened.

"Anyway, I came home to ask for Dad's forgiveness. I remembered something I did when we were at The Red Top. Remember that place?"

Her brother nodded. The Red Top was a diner the Roan family used to eat in every second week when their mother would get paid. Mom and Dad always ordered cheeseburgers and root beer floats for the kids and blue plate specials for themselves.

"The Red Top. Man, I haven't thought about that place in years," said Don.

"It's still the same. Jukeboxes are still there," she said.

They smiled at one another remembering that a quarter could buy three songs. Mom and Dad picked one each but the kids always fought over which of them would choose the final song.

Sandra continued, "I said something one night that changed him. I remember that after that night, Dad was different."

Don took out a crumpled pack of American cigarettes, taking two out, lighting them and offering Sandra one. Although not a regular smoker, she shrugged and took it.

"Mom and I made fun of him. Remember how proud he

always was about being Blackfoot. He wanted us to know so much but Mom, she never let him teach us anything. Remember?"

It was silent as they both smoked for awhile.

His voice tight, Don answered, "Yeah, I remember how she used to yell at him about being a goddamn Indian when he spoke the language."

Suddenly the voice changed, "You know what? He used to teach me anyway. I mean, I had to promise never to say them in front of Mom. Of course, I've learned to speak it pretty good now," he said glancing over shyly.

His smile broke the tension. Sandra returned it with a brief one of her own and began again.

"Anyway, Dad was trying to talk to us about War Mountain. I remembered picking up her Coke bottle, pretending to take a drink then slurring some awful thing about being Dad falling off the mountain if he ever went up."

Don took a final drag. The cigarette butt flew away in a tiny red arc when he flicked it. Sandra ground hers out.

"You know something, I'm wiped. I can't talk about this anymore. Can we go?" she murmured.

"Sure, sis. C'mon I'll drive. We'll take your little putter. I can get the pickup tomorrow," he motioned to the truck beside them.

Sandra looked back at the bar. "Dad'll be okay?" she asked.

"Don't worry about him. I'll take care of him," he answered.

Her brother's calmness reassured her. Since they'd left the bar, she'd been afraid; afraid of being with her father. There was much to be said but Sandra felt ready now.

"We've got a place on the base of the mountain. It's his Grandmother's old house," her brother said while getting in the car.

Sandra put her head on his warm shoulder. The buildings

on either side of the street were squat and forlorn, but their signs looked new. As they drove down the single paved road through town, every one of the four traffic lights turned green as the car approached.

Heather Harris

Coyote and the Anthropologist

Coyote was walking along
When he came upon a man who obviously wasn't from here.
The man said, "Ah, Coyote, I've been asking these Elders
About the nature of Coyote.
I am attempting to write the definitive work on the Coyote character."

Coyote wasn't sure what "definitive" was but he said
"Well, I should be able to help you with that.
Coyote is the exponent of all human possibilities.
He embodies the moral ramifications of our thought processes.
And he actualizes the dichotomous relationship between man and nature."

The anthropologist was impressed.
He had a brilliant career-enhancing thought.
"Coyote, how would you like to co-author a paper with me
And come up to the university to present it at a scholarly conference?"

Coyote thought about it for a minute
"Yes," he said, "I will."

Well, Coyote and the anthropologist went to the big city to the big university.
They worked on that paper until it was perfected.
The anthropologist was really excited and anxious,
Looking forward to the awe and admiration of his colleagues.
It was such a coup to actually have Coyote there to co-present the paper.

The day of the conference came.
The anthropologist had arranged to present last
To increase the anticipation.
Coyote listened to the first presenter.
He fidgeted through the next one.
He snoozed though the next one.
And half way though the fourth one
He whispered to the anthropologist
He was going to he bathroom.

Heather Harris

The scholars droned on and on
But Coyote didn't return.
The anthropologist was getting worried
When suddenly there was a commotion outside the room.
The anthropologist went to see what was going on.

He found the buffet table in ruins
Coyote muzzled prints in every dish.
He encountered a matronly female colleague
With Coyote paw prints on the butt of her dress.
He found a big pile of stinking, steaming Coyote shit in the middle of the floor
And no Coyote to be seen.

At last, the anthropologist understood the true nature of Coyote.

Heather Harris

The Question of Cousins

Everybody knows that all Indians are cousins. And it's surprising to find out how often that's really true. I'm sure if any two Indians who meet laid down enough genealogy they'd find out exactly how they are cousins or auntie and nephew or uncle and niece or some other kin relationship. I started thinking about this when I discovered the other day that one of my favourite students is related. Now Jaalen's Haida and I didn't think I had any Haida relatives of any sort. Well, as these things usually go, I was at his dad's place when he introduced me to his cousin whose mother was from Kispiox. It turns out that my student's cousin's mother was my ex-husband's cousin – a pretty close relationship in Indian terms. So now Jaalen can call me "Auntie" like half my other students do as well as nearly everybody in Kispiox under the age of thirty.

A few days later a bunch of us were having a discussion about proper and improper marriages. In societies with clan systems like the Haida, Gitxsan and others, one must marry outside their own clan. This is called "clan exogamy" in anthropologist parlance. To marry within one's clan is called "*gaats*" (incest) by the Gitxsan. I don't know what the Haida call it other than bad form. We argued about what percentage of Haida and Gitxsan have married appropriately. And we argued about what really constitutes a proper marriage because marriage within one's clan is not the only issue.

Every young Aboriginal person, from the first day of the onset of puberty has heard a million times from their mother /aunite/grandmother, "You can't go out with him/her, he/she is your cousin." Young people dread hearing this. When a young Aboriginal person sees an attractive member of the opposite sex, they say a little prayer that goes something like this, "Thank you, Creator, for putting this wonderful person before me, and please, God, don't let them be my cousin."

I figure at puberty all young people should be issued a genealogy chart with all ineligible marriage partners crossed off with a big X. The young person in search of a partner could then mark off other no longer potential eligibles as they marry/move away/die/come out of the closet/etc. Pretty soon most would be down to those claiming only borderline sanity and those with more bad habits than good.

Anyway, returning to the issue of who is and who is not an eligible marriage partner, the big question seems to be, if everyone of your generation is your cousin, then who can you marry? Well, the answer is, that you marry your cousin. What? I've been told over and over and over, I can't marry my cousin! Well, that's true and not true. You can, in fact, marry your cousin as long as you marry the right kind of cousin. As a matter of fact, in some cultures, you are supposed to marry your cousin. Marriages between biologically close cousins (like first and second) don't seem to be encouraged but marriages with third, fifth and eighth cousins often are. How does that work? Well, for example, in societies that recognize kin matrilineally like the Haida and Gitxsan, all cousins on your mothers side, no matter how far removed, are considered brothers and sisters and are, therefore, needless to say, forbidden. However, because your mother and father had to be different clans to marry and you belong to your mother's clan, then members of your father's clan are eligible marriage partners. Get it? Well, it's easy for us to understand and that's all that matters. While it may not be obvious to those from outside the community who don't know who belongs to what clan, for those inside the community, the person with a gaats marriage might as well have a scarlet "G" emblazed on their forehead.

Now, to sum up, all Indians are cousins but we are not doomed to extinction because there are right cousins and wrong cousins. If you come from a matrilineal society your paternal cousins are right cousins and your maternal cousins are wrong cousins. if you come from a patrilineal society it's the other way around. Oh, oh, if you come from a bilateral society and everybody is your real cousin, what happens then? I'll leave that for them to sort out.

Reflection

Debby Keeper

See

See them in mirrors
Figures on glass
See their reflection
Shadows they cast

Islands of solitude
Watch without sight
Without understanding
Ask for what's right

A glimpse within
And what did they see
Eyes cast downward
No longer to be…

Reveal the darkness
Stand naked with shame
Passed through tobacco
Leave you their pain

Offer a prayer
Hope they are well
Ask for the strength
Despair not to dwell.

Debby Keeper

I want to feel…

I want to feel…

the rain

the sound of rolling thunder in the distance
white hot lightning as it sears the ground,
burns through the protective barriers to the flesh
droplets and then torrents of cool, clean water
against tired, unadorned skin
wash away, take away those scars of time
visions of horror and feelings of pain.

Debby Keeper

i am

well yes,
i am part indian
i got the nose
and a treaty card
drink jar after jar
of strong dark teas
i like my bannock hard
driving a big old car
but i've never eaten beaver
or jellied moose nose
hmm...

well... no
i don't play bingo
nevadas
any type of scratch & win card
no VLT's
don't drink Pepsi
or like KFC
don't spend too much time drinking
or hanging out in bars
only dark in summer
and got no relatives
currently working for the government
and i've never eaten dog
(maybe on dog feast).

Jack Forbes

In the Dunes

My eye-lids were closed
to mark the dunes
and the little hollows,
the pools
and to see better
the wind
which in itself is not seen
and it came to me.

Wet it was
mist my cheeks
the smell was strong
of sea-things
as I lay back
and drifted.

And then ant-thoughts I had
because it seemed
the sand was no longer smooth
I looked at the mountains
of boulders
round-ended here
and jagged there
and I could not lay upon these rocks
as big as me.

But imagine
strong I was
and I could lift one
almost as big as me
and move it
my own piles making
here and there.

Jack Forbes

The Dune was neither smooth nor soft
not at all
a rough rock-slide it was
the top reaching to Heaven
and on many legs
I articulated across glittering jewels
moving seeds
beneath dune grass
tall as Giant Redwoods
and to climb straight up
was for me an easy thing.

A presence I could feel
wind-brought
and my eyes opened
to a grayness which moved
in swirls
and I was not anywhere that I had
thought before.

It was cool
but it was not cold
and there were no sounds
the surf flattened to silence
or had it left
the ocean now around me was one
where sky moved in undulating swells.

Sitting down where I was
I bathed myself with mist
and being clean
I scattered tobacco
and laying back
I began to float.

Jack Forbes

At a certain moment
a bright light bathed me
but then I was in grayness
and then light again
and whiteness all below
not wanting to go higher
I lay there on the top of
foam piled up like snow
and rounded into half-circles
and wisps of shapes
and it was all whiteness
and blue above.

I played with the cloud there
and it was wet
and in motion
and I knew that things are
made in clouds
that clouds listen
and call
in their own way
and prayers they hear
but powerful they are
and playful
and being strong
but when they roll together
with the wind in games
one cannot being human
play with them.

Floating there
my mind cloud-thoughts had
and I could see
and understand
to roll and roll

Jack Forbes

and swim in the air
and to swirl together
in great masses
rising high like a great
white giant
crashing about making
thunder and lightning
frightening creatures
with the power given by the Creator.

The pride I could feel
not arrogance but pride
in cloud-knowing-itself
the parent of life below
plants and animals
the earth-mother waiting
to be wettened.

Capricious they are not
these clouds I learned
prayers they hear
but the games they play
and with the wind
they must be free
they cannot be fast-chained
free to be without routine.

Not out of meanness do they
pour themselves upon the Earth
more than people want
or less than people want
not out of meanness but
because of the winds and
the power they must play out.

Jack Forbes

And there I could feel the softness
but the power beneath
tense it was
and growing
and must be used
layer upon layer
of muscles of mist
so soft each water drop
and linked so hard
roaring like a great buffalo
bull across the skies
yellow eyes flashing
and the bang!

Rough it is but soft in love
like falling snow-flakes
and water droplets
touching Mother Earth
and there I became like
a snowflake ribbed as a basket
patterned so
and floating like a little white raft
rocking downwards.

And into Mother Earth
I sank
a spot of wetness
I became and downward
descending in her crevices
porous she was
as I went
into softness
all softness
and darkness it was.

Jack Forbes

And I could taste her there
and her taste of earth became me
and I became her
and it was good.

How long I lay within her
I know not
and then a pull I felt
a gentle sucking
pulled me
so gently
was I pulled
and I knew a root
was calling me
and I went squeezing in
as fluid moves.

I became then a part of that plant
moving upwards
slowly upwards
up the stalk of that plant
green I was
I could feel greenness
for green I had become.

Warmer I was
Sun I could see
green it was
and then it was bright
blue sky
and upwards I was flying.

Backward I looked and there
that dune grass I saw
the one Giant as a Redwood

Jack Forbes

when I was ant-size
now small again
tiny and disappearing
into the shape of the dune
and the dune becoming
only a haze
as higher I went
to the Cloud-World
again.

So good I felt
that water I wanted
to be forever
a cloud to belong to
and an ocean
a sea
running rapids
in a river skimming past trout
and minnows.

I felt then that
waterdrops and clouds
have such great knowledge
for
sooner or later
a drop will pass through
the inside of
everything
becoming truly a part of
the earth even the rocks
all living creatures
the sky
the sea.

Jack Forbes

I awakened on the dune
with the morning sun
of an unrecorded day
and I offered tobacco
and washing my body
with its light,
seeing that I possessed
a long shadow
I saw that I
was not yet water only.

I knew then the words of a song:
There is a sacred path
through the Dunes
It cannot be seen
There is a sacred path
through life
it cannot be seen

but good it feels
to touch upon it
happy it feels to
know it is there.

Jack Forbes

Suspended Animation

Suspended animation
Frozen
Icy hard
Unmoving
Tropical hurricanes screeching through veins
thick with frost.

Cool to people's touch
Professing nothing-
Cold steel frame giving deceptive form to
molten matter.

Marshmallow-like dropping downward to the
soles of my feet
Leaving dry empty-places echoing hollowly
like a suit of armor
standing in an empty
castle hall.

I fear my
Hot inside
Will seep out
Leaving me
Totally emptied.

What I feel inside-
What I can do
Two extremes, two minds, two hearts, pounding
against each other –
Parallel lines
must never meet – but
Mine do.

Jack Forbes

Stranger within –
Which one is me?
Will winter win and hold me rigid,
or perhaps I'll be warm and soft
Or maybe yet
Searing torrents
will spew forth in
Sudden acts.

The chemistry of
My being has not been studied yet.
Strange elements
Undiscovered
Coffined out of sight while still alive
Suffocating,
entombed,
but not yet dead.

Authentic life
Demands
That I unveil myself –
But not in some public place
Classified and put in a tidy box of
stereotyped assumptions
By whisperers, hands over mouths,
head turned aside to cover
their foul breath.

I will chip ice away with my own
Chisel
Peeling off the armor
Upon my chosen ground
Feeling the heat of unity and
Lusty life
as it should be
Reflected in my own

Jack Forbes

Mirror.
Subversion of established order
Castle ramparts must not echo with the
screams of hollow statues
Suddenly hot with life
swords upraised to
Shout out sounds of truth.

Teachers
Bosses
Many guardians
Have tried so hard
So mightily
To turn me into soft stone of which they
can carve and shape
Approved images
Pedestaled and on display
amid
Antique pots and urinals.

Indians, though, are
Hard to form
Haven't you heard that yet?
Blow torch hearts will burn the hands
of those who try to mold-
Beware
if I explode.

To be a
Free man
Is my flame;
I see its reflection behind
my eyes
And I, a warning give-
It grows stronger.

Jack Forbes

Suspended animation-
but under the shroud of deceptive form
Muscles flex and
Juices flow
And like a butterfly cocooned
I prepare eagerly
to
appear.

Jack Forbes

Getaway

Getaway
In dark tunnels
Running
Twisting
Slipping
Watching for a light
Stopping
Listening for footsteps
In dark holes
Spaces between things
Cracks
Small places
Hiding momentarily
Sharp angles against my back
No rest here
Getaway
Making my getaway.

Getaway
You tell me
Why am I running
Like a deer
Leaping fences
Behind bushes when a car goes by
Whose behind those headlights
Fierce eyes so red
Panting
Running
Shirt soaking wet
And dirty
Crawling under cars
Old houses
Black widows don't scare me

Jack Forbes

Half as much
Tight crawl spaces
Heading for openings
Getaway
I have to get away.

They tied my hands
Tried to
But I'm hard to tie down
Confidently
Feverishly
Unknotting knots
Slipping loose
Slipping out
No noose tonight
Yelling and screaming
They thought I ran up the stairs
But I disappeared
Into old foundations
Of liberty
On my belly
In the dirt
Crawling for a
Getaway.

Getaway
In the darkness
Of the night
Cold, so cold
They took my money
No coat
Running along side streets
Back alleys
All alone now
This is the moment I trained for

Jack Forbes

All these years
Studying
Preparing for
My getaway.

Getaway
Over fences
Hearing my heart
My smell
Telling dogs
I'm running with them
Dog-catchers
I have no license
To be here anymore
No right
To exist
It has been decided
Annulled
By decree
Nothinged
Not supposed to be
Making my
Getaway.

Getaway
From arrogant fools
To the hills or to
Stay in the city
A Black woman
Gives me mean looks
And a dime
For a cup of coffee
To keep me warm
It was a cold night
I'm sure I looked dirty

Jack Forbes

Strange
Like a man
On a
Getaway.

Getaway
Miles away
Coming out of holes
In the ground
Like a gopher coming up
At night
Surfacing to
Look around
Sniffing the air
Smelling enemies
Sliding back
Out of sight
On my
Getaway.

Getaway
Leaving friends behind
Memories
No time to ache yet
Life is still the question
No tears for those
Never to be seen again
Reputations lost
Turning that last tunnel
Not to be found
Detested or mourned
Who knows
No time to think on one's
Getaway.

Jack Forbes

Getaway
Down the Mind's millionth channel
Passageways so dark
Unexplored asylums
Traps perhaps
Stumbling over purposes long
Forgotten
Impulses charging
In opposite directions
Clotting
Vision
Blindness and brilliance
Genius gone astray?
What fools can make a clean
Getaway.

Getaway
From one's own paranoia
Are pursuer's real
Really there
Or just demons
Of the dream
Is this my own chase
After myself
Around in circles
Strange neighbourhoods
Factory brick walls
And dead ends
Eight-to-five
Streets
Offering no
Getaway.

Getaway
Damn I have to-

Can't stay and be
Murdered
Annihilated
Desecrated
I'm not going to lay there and be raped
Over
And
Over
By masked creatures with uniforms
of sodden sameness
Leering down at me
No more
No more
Find me
Yes I'll find me a
Getaway.

Getaway
Escape from sanity
What is sane in a
Place where everything
Ends up in a
Sewer
Including one who is
On his
Getaway.

Getaway
If I can make the hills
Hitching rides on
Strange boulevards
Watching for
Dangers
Behind billboard signs
Hiding

Jack Forbes

My own face
With smiles
And reassurance
I'm okay friend
Just on my
Getaway.

Getaway
Will you help or
No, you have forgotten me
Already
My name, what is it,
Already gone from your lips
Erased just
That fast
How fickle but no,
I wasn't real anyway
Fictional character
Invented
For laughs
And now, well now,
He's on his
Getaway.

Getaway
From a place where lies
Are truth and truth
Is all lies
Don't you see
Police strut
Don't you see
Ready to move
On me
I had to go
It was time

Jack Forbes

Just barely
To go to the hills
I know the hills
I'll be there soon
On my
Getaway.

Getaway
Gone away
Yes he's gone away they'll say,
Just ran off
Forget him
He didn't matter
No loss you see
He'll be erased,
From your thoughts
No troubling you
With memories
No reminders staring at you
With big rat eyes
Gnawing, no none of that
On his
Getaway.

Getaway
Zig-Zag, here and there
Sharp turns to deceive
Laughter fools them
Clowns do get away
Lunatics too
There are many ways to
Getaway.

Getaway
Along trails my mind has

Jack Forbes

Plotted out for just this
Occasion,
My friend don't worry about me
Because you can be damn
Sure
I'll
Getaway.

Charles L. Mack

**Repo Cowboys
Down the Highway Maniac**

Nothing ever goes quite as planned. We learn that the roads of life can take many twined and unsought turns. Planned destinies can be turned upside down and inside out. Our choices may be deemed with principle and thoughtful insight but the end product may be a corkscrew of a ride. At times like these we realize that we are still in full search of infinite wisdom. I appreciate with the utmost gratitude the human experience bequest on me by a maniac cowboy. He was an outlaw, a con man, a boss, a perfect conversationalist, both good and evil; there was never a dull moment in the art of repossessing cars.

We didn't go after the junk. Cadillacs, four-wheeled drive pickups, sports cars, RVs, sedans and a few semis; these were our meal tickets to a monthly paycheck. New car repossession was by far the elite of this unpopular trade. Mollimer Shagnafty was the short and stocky cowboy type. He had rigged up an old trailer house frame for use as a car trailer and beefed up his motor in his two-wheeled drive pickup. Mollimer was always a man on a mission and he approached every project with such focus and seriousness. It was the spring of 1997 and Mollimer, a trailer court neighbour, came to me with an offer that was hard to refuse. The stage was set for change.

Working with the Rosebud Sioux Tribe was getting to be a complete burnout and the jagged cuts from tribal politics demoralized my stance on staying strong in the face of outright stupidity. The implements of defense I dropped and the next course of action I felt was close at hand; there had to be a way out. It was through neighbourly talk that Mollimer learned of my yearning to break from the depths of tribal employment and government.

Mollimer, a white man himself, was cleaning up on a small car repossession contract with a car dealership out of Rapid City, SD. and informed me of his upcoming expansion and the need for an employee. Mollimer was a cowboy with many connections and he connected on a gold mine. Mollimer was that type, as he would listen to people while visiting and ask questions and get information. His last job with the car dealership in Rapid City connected him with an automobile financing company out of Florida. These people in Florida did the actual financing of contracts at major dealerships across the country. Once Mollimer was in contact with these corporate types, things started to roll. With a repossessed BMW sports car we headed to Oklahoma to visit with the heads of one of the financing company's branch office. Mollimer was smooth and surprised them by taking them out for dinner and that same night he bedded down one of the finance company employees. He even went out of his way and sent the ailing president of the company roses and Black Hills gold while she was in the hospital.

Tribal employment soon ended for me and I enrolled into the *University of Car Repossession*. Mollimer agreed to pay me every week the same salary as my last job. Soon, one of Mollimers' small trailer house rooms was converted into a high tech office. There was a fax machine, fancy new phone, a word processor, file cabinet, desk and chairs, and last but not least, posters of deer and naked women.

One of his first contracts came with a $30,000 check and Mollimer cashed it and brought it over to show me. There we stood by his pickup and in a large envelope were stuffed $30,000 in *frog hides*. This financing company looked into Mollimer's past work around the state and learned of his high success and upon so sent the money up front. Mollimer waved the cash in my face and informed me that we had our work cut out for us. The average cost of repossessing a car was about $5,000. One of our first jobs called for the repossession of six cars. We brought these cars in from all over the Mid-west and upon doing so, there were more contracts and big, fat money.

We just kept hitting the highway, with bags of clothes and cash. Soon Mollimer bought a brand-new 1997 Dodge Duel Wheel pickup and a matching two car trailer. How I remember him paying for these items in total, well exceeding $45,000. And if that wasn't enough there were all the accessories that could be added. Mollimer paid cash for chrome grill guards, windshield visor, top of the line pin striping, railing, fog lights, CD player and speakers and a bed liner. Every item purchased for his pickup was the best of quality and money was no object.

Along with a decent vehicle to work out of, there was the fast food to consume in the daytime and the finest cuisine laid out in many an evening, in fine restaurants. Mollimer spared no expense on the fine dining, as he let me order anything that the establishments could offer. There were the western clothing stores that he loved so much and the sky was the limit for purchased fashion. Mollimer even dressed me in western attire and upon doing so I learned to appreciate such clothing. Through it all I refused to wear a cowboy hat; oh how Mollimer tried converting me to *western*. Anything medical he would pay for and that included an eye test at a shopping mall. These medical checkups seemed strange because in the past, as my whole life had been spent, I would always be sitting in an Indian Health Service facility waiting for the doctor.

Through this quest of investigation and learning to read body language, we got car after car and took them to the nearest big town auto auction. And from the beginning, Mollimer was a man with a medical problem, sadly *he* had diabetes. He read up on the disease and learned every aspect he could about it. So, in free time we walked and exercised and I watched Mollimer become more and more of a vegetarian. He loved to eat the cow but learned to divert to other types of meat, including fish.

I became a repo man, cowboy type and also a highway

nurse. Day after day his finger had to be pricked and blood tested with a portable blood sugar unit. Then there were the syringes and small bottles of insulin. Sometimes his vision would blur on him and I had to take the wheel.

Enter the bar scene and gloom and doom of success. Mollimer was all cowboy and rightfully so. He came from a strong family background of hats, boots and bullshit. The western bars and dance clubs became his *rest and relaxation*, if you want to call it that. There wasn't much rest and relaxation experienced in these cowboy bars. Whiskey nights with twang-twang music and there I sat soberly on a bar stool watching my boss *cowboy up*. There were the Montana bars, New Mexico saloons and the Oklahoma western clubs. Of all the bars I sat in, Oklahoma bars by far had some of the most beautiful women in the world. All in all there I sat, a non-drinker, in an environment full of smoke, booze, wild rednecks and thousands of women. At times I felt like Ghandi, doing my best to control the lust.

Many a night was spent with Mollimer and his *hand picked* woman of the night in a motel room. I would lay there alone in one bed, in total darkness and the stench of booze and crotches and sounds of sexual activity came from the other bed. Mollimer didn't care whom he brought to his room and I just lay there in my bed and tried to ignore it all. He always laughed about it the next morning, then he would get crabby about the days work ahead.

The roads got longer and the nights deepened. Mollimer became dependent on drugs to stay awake and how I remember how he changed while under the influence. In his comatose state of mind he felt alone and at times would try to entice me to join his spaced out world. It was during these tripped-out tours he would take that Mollimer would open up his world to me; a somewhat troubled one at that. The darkened road trips made my mind feel like a suspended brain, as he would tell me his life stories. Staring into the darkness with an endless yellow line moving under the pickup and listening to his tribulations. A product of bitch baby syndrome and the pain of not knowing his real father. The family torment he carried, as he never got along with his mother very well. He betrayed his grandparents a time or two. He was divorced and admitted to being a womanizer.

Once while we went deer hunting on his grandparents' land, he took me to a small hill. He drove to the base of the hill and we got out and walked to the top. There was a weathered out hole at the peak. Mollimer stared at the hole with little emotion and then explained its presence. It was his own hand dug grave and he explained how he was going to rig up a contraption that would automatically bury him once he blew his head off with a .270 deer rifle. But, that was over five years ago. He informed me and since he has come to grips with himself. I stared at the crater and was not shocked because I felt he was lunatic fringe. We then commenced to jump back into his pickup and finished up the day's hunting.

Many a time Mollimer, court judges and myself would sit in chambers and discuss car financing. It was strange because we would take some of our cases to court and would win every time. When people haven't made a car payment in over a year, it becomes quite obvious that all their bullshitting doesn't hold up well in court. Afterwards some Judges would sometimes ask us for help in getting a good car deal somewhere. Mollimer also bedded down a clerk of courts for awhile. After awhile I could tell whom he would have in the sack that night. How I recall the countless calls on his cell phone that were from his various female contacts.

Mollimer did have his little sparks of nobleness and this was cast down on him when we went to repossess a car from an older couple. The elderly man was recovering from cancer treatment and the wife kept care of him. The old couple lived in the country and while interviewing them it was obvious that there was hardship. I can still see Mollimer coming out of their house, standing in their yard and gazing across the neighbouring cornfield. Mollimer in a faint voice looked at me and told me that we were going to let this one go. He made the connotation of having some morals. He then grabbed the brim of his cowboy hat and went through the motion of straightening it out and then he told me that we were leaving. We never did go back to that place.

The repossession of cars got old after about five months and it was tiring for me. Mollimer had a new girlfriend and every time they went out, he thought I had to go. Things weren't the same anymore. Bars, parties, long nights and longer days. Work was suffering and Mollimer was in some type of non-describable love. I didn't mind him splurging on his wench, but when it cut into my salary, it became a problem. The suffering of work started to irritate my cowboy boss and he would take out his hangover frustrations on me. That type of ridicule soon turned to torture and there had to be a way out.

I didn't argue with the man very much. This cowboy was stout. He had a temper and was known to have hit a man in the head and knock him out with just one punch. He respected me somewhat and I don't think he would have tried this, but I took no chances. Upon knowing my wish to leave this employment, Mollimer became quiet. He confessed that he wasn't perfect and tried to keep me on as an employee, but he also knew I was leaving regardless of what he could say or do.

It wasn't a surprise to find out that my last paycheck had a stop payment issued. Strange though it seems I remained calm and collected about the situation. It was his style and even though I relied on this last pay installment, it did not matter anymore. I was free from the bar atmosphere, the long nights and longer days, the loose women, car lot con men, screwy judges and pricking fingers for blood. No more hangover attitude from the boss or the unsightly presence of his ape-faced girlfriend and her hyena laugh. Emancipation was sweet and besides I didn't do much during my last week of employment.

Mollimer always told me that a person has to live on the edge once in awhile. I always believed that he went over the edge. Still there is an enchantment to it all. There were some aspects of freedom experienced and a human spirit opened up to me, his. Mollimer took each day as it came without worrying about the outcome of what he did. He was western and the cowboy metaphor was almost a circus in comparison. He told me his deepest, darkest and hideous secrets. He trusted me like a true friend but in the end, he must of thought that he betrayed me. Sometimes I pull out the worn and frayed $1,000 bad check and I am reminded of the wild ride of being a *repo cowboy*. Then I ponder his return home and the little hill that waits for him.

Candy Zazulak

Frogman

Frog man Evolving man
In white and black I see you
Not in balance
Body is white pure motion
Harmony of movement
But from neck up is black
Busy black full of painful blame

Frog man Warrior man
Your redhot anger
Is frozen in memory
What good is freedom of Expression
If it hurts
Yes there has been suffering
Yes Injustice
Genocide
Invasion
Expropriation
Oppression
Extermination
Others have done this
Must you add to the pain

Frog man Traditional man
Life has made you the way you are
Even to those dark smoldering churning seas that you call eyes

Frog man Good man
Peace is elusive
The truth is to love Humanity
Corrupt man will never find Peace
Those who love may find the path
Where hope suddenly summersaults into existence
Possibilities unfold
The Creator smiles
All is in balance
For now

Sandra A. Olsen

Across Many Miles

Across many miles
Across sacred land
Across many generations
Who live each day
Breathing litter
of many miles
in many plants.
What will happen
To Mother Earth who's
covered in endless litter?
Time passes us in
Sacred existence
Existence of an
ending era.

Across many miles
Across sacred land
Across many generations
Who live on
Suffering land.
crying for help.
Crying,
"Please let me breathe!
Please don't let me
scream in endless pain,
Please stop Raping me of
Natural existence."
Time passes us in
Remembrance to fulfill
Every moment we exist.

Sandra A. Olsen

Across many miles
Across sacred land
Across many generations
Who live in a
New existence.

Generations of children
Who breathe and suffer
litter in the air.
Generations of ancestors
pleading with our
Creator to stop
This endless litter.

Across many miles
Across sacred land
Across many generations
Who live each day
In suffering of sacred land.

As a Nation
We should build strength
To stop suffering
Of millions
Across millions of miles
On sacred land.
Together we'll succeed
In saving Mother Earth.

Across many miles
Across sacred land
Across many generations
Who'll remember
strength and courage
we have

Sandra A. Olsen

Strength and courage
To stop endless pain
Of natural existence.
To stop the screaming of
Miles and miles
We covered.

Across many miles
Across sacred land
Across many generations
Of yet to come
Across many Miles.

Connie Crop Eared Wolf

My Friend Tamra

She came into my life like a winter snowstorm
Like the few visible flakes that melt
As they touch the earth
As colleagues, we touched
Then like a full blown prairie blizzard
Our friendship became strong

Tamra, the *Napiaakii* with the Indian heart
Pow-wow dancer
Your travels are many
Your path unique
You came into my life like a prairie snow storm
Calming the restlessness, that entered my home

Tamra, the *Napiaakii* with the Indian Heart
Your spirit was captured and brought to the prairies
Like the chinook, Alvin
Strong wind from the west, melting your heart
Exposing the fertile soil of your personality
You embraced and lived the life of a true Blood woman

My friend Tamra
Scholar, speaker of truth
Teacher, mentor to the young
You see the potential of young Blood children
Expanding their ideals, encouraging their growth
Planter of wisdom in fertile minds

Tamra, winter blizzard
Storm from the east
You came into my life
Gentle, pow-wow dancer
You enriched my life, with your laughter
You warmed my heart with your friendship

Theresa G. Norris

Maria

A long time ago in a very large cold country there lived a very small girl. The small girl did not live alone; she lived in a large family with many many brothers and sisters including a mother and a father. The small girl was not too poor but not too rich either. Her favorite food was toast soaked in milk sprinkled with plenty of sugar. Every morning she woke up out of a deep sleep and wished that she could sleep longer knowing that the moment would come when she had to put her little feet out from under the warm cozy blankets onto the icy frozen floor of her room. Many times she could have sworn she felt frost nipping at her heels and toes. She hated those little teeth. The small girl also had a name, her name was Maria.

Maria lived from day to day as everyone does, she did not have an unusual life. At least not unusual in the eyes of the world nor in the eyes of her many brothers and sisters or her mother and father. For all intents and purposes Maria was just another ordinary girl with a taste for sugar. She never got into trouble, she knew how to spell and learned to count. Though a faint realization was beginning to grow in her thoughts and perhaps Maria did have a problem, a problem even she did not notice at first. One day she noticed her busy family bustling about her. She noticed them all rushing about speaking loudly amongst each other. She noticed that not one person in her family noticed her. Gradually, she noticed that she was invisible.

At first there was no reason for her to suspect that she was different from the other members of her family. Eventually the signs of her transparency became clear to her. At first the signals were faint and soon enough the truth was revealed to her. Often she would hear her mother's worried voice wondering where all of that sugar was disappearing to and secondly when she heard her brothers complaining that there was no toast left in the house, and where did it go? And then when she decided to move out of her house to under her bed, not a single person noticed. To Maria this was enough proof to confirm her suspicion. She moved about the house like a fading shadow. Counting the number of times people did not notice her, reciting the letters of their names.

Maria took to wearing an emerald green chiffon dress; she thought the translucent hue was flattering to her invisibility. She also found an old pair of tap dancing shoes with hard silver crests attached with tiny nails to the bottoms of the heels and toes. The shoes were faded black leather but she loved the black satin ribbons that secured them to her little feet. When she marched through the rooms of the large family home the silver crests of the shoes made small tapping sounds like elves hammering leaves of gold. She wondered why nobody ever complained. She wondered if invisible girls in tap dancing shoes could be heard. She wondered if sounds have shadows.

One day as Maria was clicking through her house in and out of every room she noticed an open door in the kitchen, a door that led to the garden. She peered out of the door and noticed the sun was shining very brightly, she noticed that far away at the very back of the garden there stood a tree, a very beautiful tree. A tree with bright green leaves almost as green as her dress. The tree was sprinkled with shiny red cherries. The cherries reminded her of millions of ruby earrings tugging at the green ears of the tree.

Without hesitation Maria whisked herself out of the back door and down a path that brought her to the tree, she ran so quickly that her little shoes forgot to make a sound. So enticing was the tree. Out of breath and slightly awed by her discovery all she could do was bend her neck back and gaze up at the tree. Home she thought, I have found myself a new home, not that she had been looking for a new home of course but such was her wonderment. Maria noticed a ladder leaning on the trunk of the tree, a convenient coincidence for just as quickly as Maria scurried down the path to reach the tree she hopped onto the ladder and up into it's heart. Mercifully the tree accommodated her shiny slippery shoes by its strong level branches and many stairs like knots.

Under a canopy of leaves Maria saw the maze like structure of branches and she smelled the soft sweet scent of ripe cherries. The sun shone through openings where gnarled branches separated, Maria realized that she was in the center chamber of the tree. It had never occurred to her before that behind all of those leaves that trees could probably be hollow. Absorbing the scene before her with its scent and light Maria thought perhaps she should rest her little body in one of the elbows of a branch, and possibly tuck her little head on a clump of leaves. Maria exhausted from all of her new impressions, fell asleep.

Maria dreamed about a chamber, a living room in a tree. She dreamed that she slipped out of her shoes and hung them by their black ribbons on a branch. She dreamed that a very large very shiny, black crow, almost too slippery to look at kept sliding in and out of her sleepy vision as he laid a soft blanket over her shoulders. She dreamed of the delicious aroma of cherry pie baking happily. In the distant corners of her sleep she heard the sound of tinkling teacups as they were set on a table. Her sleeping tongue regressed in her mouth at the prospect of drinking steaming tea.

Opening her eyes feeling refreshed, Maria drank in the scene around her. Before her eyes sat a large glistening black crow. The crow was sitting at a table set with steaming cups of tea and two large slices of bubbling cherry pie. The crow's feathers shone so brightly that Maria could almost see her own reflection in his wings. She was visible in those wings and it made her feel glad. Her image fluttered gently toward her as he extended a wing to invite her to his table. Smiling timidly Maria sat opposite the crow wishing that he might very kindly put three teaspoons of sugar in her tea and perhaps an extra four on top of her cherry pie, secretly she would have preferred toast.

"Do not worry," cawed the crow, interrupting her thoughts.

"I have filled each cherry with sugar before I put it in the oven and the tea is made from their juice. Feel free to add a small amount of milk, and please eat quickly young lady for my name is Ordy and we have a job to do."

"My name is Maria," said Maria as she obediently set about eating her lunch.

Absorbed by the liqueur that was her lunch, the cherry pie sang as it tickled the inside of her mouth and the tea serenaded her making her feel warm and soft. Opening her mouth to join the chorus she noticed that Ordy was no longer sitting at the table. She noticed that he was hunched over an old sewing machine. Maria noticed that all around Ordy there lay clouds of billowing silk. Silk of every colour she could possibly imagine. Maria imagined taking a little bite out of every single colour. Several shades of pink, green blue and red. Choral green turquoise and ochre. There were even colours that Maria did not know the names of. Maria pushed her chair back and slowly strolled over to where Ordy was crouched.

"Pardon me Mr. Ordy," peeped Maria, as she tested her voice, "But may I please ask you Sir what task you are busy with?"

"Hmmm," cawed Ordy. "Hmmm. I am busy making a rainbow and by the looks of it there will be a sun shower early this evening. I am very happy that you are here; I am pleased that you might help me with my task. The afternoon is growing old," cawed Ordy "and we must race with time."

Maria steadied herself and found her reflection in his wing just to be sure he was speaking to her. Feeling confident and visible Maria cleared her throat and bravely replied that she would be happy to assist but she simply had no skills that she could think of to help him. At that moment she glanced shyly at his face to see if he heard her, as she was not yet used to being heard. Ordy smiled and asked Maria if she had fingers? To which she said, "Yes I have ten fingers, ten to be exact." Behind her back she counted them just to make sure. Ordy asked her if she could use those fingers to grasp the coloured silk? Maria said, "Yes if it was not too heavy".

"Fine," replied Ordy and then in a somber caw peering directly into her eyes he asked her if she could fly? "Yes," replied Maria cautiously, "because I fit in the reflection of your wings." "Hmmm," said Ordy, "then your task will be to help me lift the rainbow high into the sky. High above the clouds. Together we will stretch it over the valley. The sun's rays will embrace it and shine through it and every living person and beast shall behold it."

"It is time now," said Ordy, "the hour to place the rainbow up into the heavens has come. I smell that soon the rain will end. Come Maria, come, the sky is waiting!"

Maria picked up her shoes by their satin ribbons and Ordy snatched his cowboy hat from a peg. He rolled the rainbow into a tight ball and led Maria through and up corridors of branches and stairs. At a certain moment Ordy reached above his head and unhooked a small brass latch. Miraculously he pushed open a square door and they climbed out of his home. Blinking at the glare of daylight Maria realized that she was standing at the very top of the cherry tree.

Maria barely had time to tie her shoes when she noticed that Ordy was extending a corner of the rainbow toward her. She stood up to take hold of the rainbow and when she touched the fabric with her fingers she was so startled by the texture that she almost lost her balance on the top of the cherry tree. For the rainbow was not made of silk it was not made of anything that she could recognize. It was warm but soft, it was lighter than a feather and if she held it too tight her fingers would sink through it's fabric. On the other hand if she did not grasp tight enough the rainbow would slip through her fingers like grains of sand or perhaps like crystals of sugar.

"This is like waking in a dream!" exclaimed Maria in a voice that she did not know she had. Ordy spread his wings to their fullest breadth and Maria found her reflection in the glossy reflection of Ordy's feathers. Extending first her right arm and then her left, Ordy swept her up into the sky, Maria's breath feared the flight and stayed atop the tree becoming a small breeze tickling the leaves of the cherry tree. At each instant Maria's reflection grew in the fine black feathers. Maria became Ordy's heart, a heart outlined by the body of a crow. Maria looked down from the sky as the distance between her Ordy and the earth grew, she could see the cherry tree growing smaller, not too far from the cherry tree stood her family home and it too grew in reverse to the size of a pin head just a speck hardly a memory. The rainbow unfurled as Maria and Ordy crossed over the horizon. Together they flew for thousands of years, years that were only seconds long and years that took forever. Maria became Ordy and Ordy reassured her with joy. The rainbow refreshed their thirst and whenever she became hungry Maria took just a small bite out of their colours.

"One day," said Maria, "we may have to go home to create another rainbow."

She enjoyed being visible.

Brent Peacock-Cohen

Frustration

Standing in a puddle
Which is endless
"There are Indian people on the shore"
Says the Raven
But I see nothing

Trudging in a desert
Which is endless
"There is an Indian village on the edge"
Says the Coyote
But I see nothing

Sitting in a longhouse
The longtables filled with Indians
the room is silent
nothing is said, not a peep
Until the food is late

An Indian in an office
listening to other people
Doing for other people
Writing for other people
While their Nation sits one short

Who says the tipi is not as good as the wheel?

William George

Squamish Floods

The ink spills, the pen bleeds, and in a good way, I shall share the teachings.

I bleed	
words	tears
barnacle wounds	ocean
to pray	flow
ancient	mountain
blood	stream

The Squamish people have
swi-OME-tun (Indian doctors), *qua-Tsay-its* (Sorcerers), and
us-YOH (Prophets).

Swi-OME-tun are the ones who heal the people,
hearts and minds made strong.

    (Indian Doctors, oh you must mean that Native rap group)

The *qua-Tsay-its* has power in medicine chants and words
and songs, knows hidden ways to use Indian paints.

    (Sorcerer, he is that WWF wrestler enit?)

The *us-YOH* sees the future and predicts what will happen to a person.

    (like the psychic hotline)

life-lines	blood	wolf dream
is river	flows	carved
surging	soil to	bedded rock
mountain stream	water	breaks
cedar	through	language
canoes	amber shores	breath

William George

A long time ago there was a great flood.
Many people died.
The Squamish people in the 21st century are forgetting
that their ancestors lived and died in the great flood.

Yes, from the slopes of Whistler Mountain
to the streets of Vancouver and North Vancouver,
Squamish people are forgetting to respect each other,
and forgetting the teachings of the old ones.

red	tears	bloodied
mountain	searching	stone
bursts	rain	cuts
terrain	drops	pushes
deep	and	river
valley	moves	claws
breaks	the	earth
through	language	surging
rock and soil	ocean	breath

And in their forgetting,
they dismiss the coming of a new prophet.
In the 21st century,
the old ones say
"listen to the one who wield the pen."

As the *swi-OME-tun*
transformed by the western society medicine,
As the *qua-Tsay-its*
transformed by technology,
As the *us-YOH* and the stories about prophecies
become transformed into fairy tales,
the Squamish people need to remember to respect.

William George

The people stop helping each other
and stop respecting the words of the old ones.
Spawning stops, salmon die.
Growing stops, berries and plants die.

The Poet like the *us-YOH* before him
tells and re-tells the story of the great flood.
He says that this disaster will happen again
if they don't change.

And the rain...
The rain this time pounds down on the people,
filling the cities and streets.
21st century rains a great flood.
This time there are
no *qua-Tsay-its* to try to stop this deluge.

bedded rock	flesh and bone
generations	soil deep
blood-line	pushes
nurtures	memory

After this flood, the landscape
and the people's mindset are transformed
so much that things do not go back to the way they were.

William George

They Rose And So Shall I

they
rose from the mountains
rose from the volcanic lava
rose from the oceans
rose from the marshes and swamps
and they were firm in their resolve to mask dance
in accordance with the first lessons

I stand here in the city
and the pull of contemporary society and traditional teachings
are massive weights applied to the foundation of who I am
blood and tears are boulders
break me through thick lines of fog and mist

I shall rise then
through the asphalt
through the sewer
the smog
the ozone
and when I gain my bearings
I will live – move here with the first dream

MariJo Moore

Atop Polacca on First Mesa

Some things are hidden in the immensity of the Arizona desert. Others are forever reappearing. As I walk across the burning sands, I feel traces of lightning that wove itself into this mesa hundreds of celebrations ago. Traces that scratch open my vision in preparation for a remarkable mystery. The hot wind sprays dust in my face, spits into my heart prayers floating in the ether for eons, and I intuitively know I will never be the same.

Today, spirits will materialize in answer to ritualistic prayers. Spirits will sing, drum and dance. The Katsinam are coming.

It is Summer Solstice, 1998. I am a visitor on First Mesa on the Hopi Reservation, invited by the Sinquah family to observe an age-old ceremony closed to non-Indians.

Consisting of approximately 4000 square-miles of arid plateaus and desert, Hopi land encompasses various dwellings which cling to the rocky cliffs of First, Second, and Third Mesas. First Mesa, barren of trees, juts out over the village of Polacca. The sky is close, turquoise, and beautiful. The mesa is colored only by sand; there is not one blade of green grass. Even the houses are sand-coloured.

"Sometimes, you focus on the black highway just to ease your eyes," Dale Sinquah tells me as we drive up the winding mountain road.

The parched earth of the desert floor is cracked open in places, showing even more dryness beneath. Yet looking down from the six-hundred-foot high mesa, I see tiny brown patches that are fields of blue corn. To my eyes, used to acres of lush green cornfields growing in a rainy Southeastern climate, seeing corn grow in this parched desert is truly a miracle.

The industrious and spiritual Hopi have managed to survive in the dry, barren desert for thousands of years. Although modern conveniences have made their way into the villages,

Hopi traditions have survived. The Hopi language is still spoken fluently, baskets are still woven from yucca plants, and celebratory traditions still have precedence. Katsinam – spirit beings who represent all aspects of universal life and live on the snow-capped San Francisco Mountains in the Cochina Forest – still come in colorful ceremony to pray for rain and abundance as they sing not just for the survival of the Hopi but for the entire world.

Traces of lightning in the sand burning feet, scratching eyes
wind spraying dust, spitting awareness
prayers bringing in respected spirits
young men on flat rooftops, standing
women with colorful shawls, sitting
children, dark and beautiful, watching

rose embroidered on loincloth of dancing Katsina
clouds, a lizard, the sun
Katsinam dancing dancing Katsinam embodying the world
the entire lost, lonely world
somewhere, far away from this plaza, children are crying
women are hurting, men are dying
all will eventually feel the prayers of dancing Katsinam
Katsinam dancing

their guttural singing tearing at my throat
splitting open my soul
taking me to a place so deep inside the sky
I may never go there again
mesmerized by movements, dreamed awake by colors
I fall deeper and deeper inside myself
than I have ever dared visit before

Young men, serious and observant, line the flat tops of the ancient stone houses. Women, reverent in their colourful shawls, sit in rows of chairs on the plaza. Children, with dark, beautiful faces, wait with ancestral anticipation for the *sine qua non*.

A slow, steady drumbeat begins to reverberate inside my heart as the plaza becomes filled with drumming, movement and color. The Katsinam are here. Singing and dancing.

This dance, like all American Indian dance, is a form of praise; a way to experience interconnectedness through motion. The art of dancing was part of life for American Indians before the conception of art ever existed. American Indian dances are beautiful metaphors for celebrating life to the fullest. Music and dance are representatives of the full range of life for American Indians. They are integral fuels that have always fed the fires of honor and traditions.

Dance is a necessary spiritual action requiring dedication and a devout sense of reverence. To dance is to pray, to pray is to heal, to heal is to give, to give is to live, to live is to dance.

Katsinam dancing dancing Katsinam are lined inside of me
celebrating not explaining celebrating the mysteries
of all interconnectedness
knowing not hoping knowing all the people need their prayers
small chosen rocks rattling inside gourds
bringing visions of cool life-giving rains
my skin erupting letting go cold chills
quickly vanishing in the hot, dry desert

Am I seeing what I am seeing?

dancing Katsinam Katsinam dancing circle never closing
eagle feathers dripping from turquoise mouths
lush green juniper surrounding singing throats
movements... gourd rattles raise upward meeting lowered faces
heads turning left
bows and arrows lowered heads following
two right steps in one place now one left now turn and repeat
singing always singing

Symbolism is more than just imagined reality to American Indians. Symbols represent spiritual reality where thought and

feeling, storyteller and story, spirit and creation, are considered the same. One need only watch a true artisan at work carving a ceremonial pipe from stone to see how ancestral spirits are present during creation. And there is no doubt evoked ancestral spirits are here within this plaza today, manifested in
in these otherworldly colorful beings.

Watching the Katsinam dance, my senses heighten as cultural chants mix with swishing rain sounds falling from gourd rattles and fill the air. Haunting, mystical sounds transport my spirit to the place inside myself where deep wounds lie hidden, and I ache for a simpler existence. The drum – its round form representing the shape of the sacred universe – emits a strong, steady heartbeat that entrances my mind and I become one with all. Agile and full of purpose, the sacred artistic dance chills my soul. I am alive.

I sit in awe of this celebratory vision and poetry births itself inside my spirit. Poetry has been the medium of mystics, prophets, and healers for thousands of years. For me, poetry is proof of the mystery living inside me; it is reality scratching at the surface of my soul; it is my true connection to the whole. Poetry is ceremony woven from the voices of the old ones, intuition, dreams and visions. The poems that find me are gifts from Spirit through me to others.

In the belief system of American Indians, this quintessential Spirit is known by many names and has many voices. These voices often penetrate our spoiled, scarred psyches and force thoughts to materialize, expressing themselves in creative forms: song, dance, music, art, literature. These creations provide us with a sense of interconnection, a sense of being. They give us proof of what we all seem to crave the most: love and hope.

Has love, like the words "sacred," "holy," and "respect" become meaningless from overuse? And what about the word hope? What is hope? Why do we need hope? What have we forgotten? With what have we lost touch? I firmly believe most people have lost touch with the land, thus they have lost touch with themselves.

To American Indians, ceremony is a necessary act to obtain or regain balance with the earth. It is the highest form of giving back to the earth so that she can replenish her supply for humankind. The purpose of ceremony is to integrate: to unite one with all of humankind and creation as well as the realm of the ancestors. Consciousness is raised and the idea of individuality shed. Ceremony brings into balance all there is.

Though each ceremony has its own special purpose which varies from nation to nation, all ceremony provides deep illumination and the realization that there is no separation from anything or anyone.

Poetry, song, art, music, and dance can help us understand this relationship, and often provides spiritual healing. Only in isolation can spiritual sickness exist, therefore, for one to heal, one must recognize a oneness with the universe.

The Cherokee story "How The Plants Gave Us Medicine" tells of a time when humans lived peacefully with the animals, were in total communication with them, and always asked the permission of the animal for its life before taking it. But when the people began to lose respect for the animals and began hunting for sport, they needlessly killed animals and destroyed the balance of the forests. Because the people forgot the importance of ceremony, the animals began to inflict diseases and infirmities upon them. The plant world, in sympathy for the people, gave their medicines as cures for the diseases. Now, this plant world is being destroyed. Since the beginning of the nineteenth century, medical science has turned its back on nature. The aspect of Spirit participating in one's healing is quickly pushed aside in favor of synthetic drugs and quick-fix therapies.

The Hopi call this *Koyaanisqatsi*, "Life out of balance; crazy life; life disintegrating; a state of life that calls for another way of living." Is life out of balance? How else can one explain the continuing destruction of the world's original forests? And the poisoning of waters, the widening hole in the ozone, the thousands of dollars spent on the excavating of bones to be examined while the problems of modern-day people continue to be ignored? What about individual lives? Are they out of balance? What about the continuing racist hate crimes, the bitter stings of discrimination and stereotyping? The rising number of suicides every year (especially among youth), the ever-present damage caused by alcoholism and drug abuse, children being born addicted and with Fetal Alcohol Syndrome, and on and on? How have we lost this important contact with our inner selves? How have we lost our connecting responsibility to each other, to the land? What have we put in the place of ceremony?

Ceremony is often shunned in favor of organized society and religion, in favor of short-cuts to spirituality, in favor of ignoring one's inner call by listening to the outer callings demanding more and more material gain. Ceremony is passed over in favor of defining instead of celebrating one's existence. In other words, we are cut off from our inner selves, from the place where we can experience spiritual connection with all there is. Shunning ceremony can cause all of life to become out of balance.

But today, atop Polacca on First Mesa, white clouds are beginning to loom in the turquoise sky, adding their celestial contribution to the celebration of the Great Mystery. And the Katsinam, poetry in motion surrounded by an aura of ceremonial certainty, dance on, singing and praying. Praying for balance to be restored to all.

> *reminding the arid earth roots of ancestral corn*
> *are resting in its ancient belly*
> *corn meal yellowed on chests*
> *corn meal leaving women's hands*
> *landing on the sacredness*
> *the blessed ageless ceremonial sacredness of*
> *dancing Katsinam Katsinam dancing*

turtle shells speaking jingling bells answering fox tails swinging
head Katsinam directing white-haired priest circling

all the people silent
I believe my heart explodes I believe my spirit takes flight
I believe my mind is touched as never before
and maybe as never again
Mudhead Katsina drumming stopping changing positions
drumming dancing turning
singing praying moaning

ho'oooooteeeee ho'te ho'te

Katsinam dancing, dancing Katsinam
dancing for all the people
dancing for all the world
stopping
leaving a changed silence
returning to the dark kiva
to pray and prepare to dance again.

The Hopi, like all American Indians, are not without factional problems. As their ancestors in the emergence stories, modern-day Hopi are still in disagreement concerning maintaining traditional beliefs or embracing progressiveness which includes acceptance of non-Hopi ways. But today, ancestral spirits are here, dancing, singing and praying. There is the collective acceptance of tradition.

I, like all the observers, am silent. Pausing in the space between knowledge and understanding. The space between wounding and healing. The space between hope and acceptance. I hear the haunting, guttural prayer-song and the accompanying sound of the slow mesmerizing drum beat. The Katsinam dance two right steps in one place, one left, turn, then repeat. These synchronized movements remind me that all is really one. That we are really a part of the all. This is truly a ceremonial celebration, truly a prayer in motion.

The human element is almost totally disregarded as the entire physical universe is recognized, revered, and celebrated. There is no attempt at explaining the universe, only at celebrating its existence. There is no cathedral, church, or temple isolating the Creator, only natural surroundings. There is no collection plate, the people give their respect and full attention. There is no preacher ranting and raving about heaven or hell, no laying on of hands, no manipulation by guilt, no Sunday-best clothing. No Tarot card readings, no channeling of the Archangel Michael. No one seeking an Indian name, performing a vision quest, or taking peyote. There is no competitive dancing, no war whoops, no clapping. Only a changed silence as the Katsinam finish their dance and head back to the darkness of the kiva, to pray and prepare to dance again.

Rainer Maria Rilke wrote, "teaching means: to ask of each person what he feels closest to in silence." As a writer, I am a teacher. And as a teacher, I am continually learning. Witnessing the metaphorical beauty of the Katsinam returning to the source of creation has deepened my silence.

As I drive across the changing desert to Phoenix to catch a flight back to North Carolina, I ask myself what I feel closest to in silence. And I hear a voice, a silvery voice wrapped in secrets of red and purple, telling me to go deep, deep inside myself. Deep to the deepest part where the light lays in the center of the darkness. That it will be here I will find the celebration of who I am, why I exist, where I come from and where I am going. And in this celebration I will find the explanation that requires no explaining, the knowledge that requires no knowing, the answer that requires no questioning. Then I would understand, and then I would not understand, and then it would not matter.

What so many of us long to know and often guess about the universe and its mystical workings, the traditional Hopi know and respect. The most important realization is to celebrate and acknowledge the Great Mystery, not try and explain. What I have experienced is pure faith. A faith that obviously exists because, after all, the Hopi still have rain and their corn still grows in the arid desert.

Bernelda Wheeler

Education is Our Buffalo

When the Department of Indian Affairs cut back on post-secondary education in 1989, protesters chained themselves in the offices and had to be bodily taken out. They were jailed, and had to go through the judicial process. I shall forever remember the day in that Saskatoon court room. We were reminded that education is a treaty right. We heard again what it has come to symbolize for Aboriginal people when Barry Ahenekew was called to the witness stand. His oration was spellbinding, eloquent and strong. Barry described the treaty signing with the belief and passion of a professional orator. The meaning of the buffalo for prairie people was articulated. We all but saw and heard the pounding of the hooves of a thousand horses as they encircled the treaty signing area. The buffalo were gone, Barry said, but their replacement could do for us as much as the thundering herds had done in their day. When he had finished his testimony, Barry stated with strength and simplicity: "Education is our buffalo."

The phrase became the title for a presentation several years later; its focus was post-secondary education. For 1993, the University of Winnipeg's distinguished chancellor's lecturer was Winona Stevenson – she, who had years earlier been in the courthouse in Saskatoon, one of the accused who were protesting cutbacks on education, the replacement for buffalo, Barry had said. The buffalo will never again be our staff of life, and education is being eroded. But, unlike the buffalo, education can be a constant and can give us what the buffalo once gave us – a rich, healthy, flourishing and balanced way of life. It can – only if the federal and provincial governments keep their part of the treaty agreements. The recent provincial government's imposition of the PST is a blatant and arrogant breach of treaty. The action tells us that Saskatchewan neither respects nor honours the treaties. Education for Aboriginal students will be maintained though – the province wants that pot of gold. Multi-millions of dollars annually are poured into the provincial piggy bank for education on our behalf from federal monies. In the meantime the most a post-secondary Aboriginal student receives for living allowance while studying is $675.00 a month. At that rate the ten million that Saskatchewan will get from us in PST every year would pay for 14,814 students to live, albeit frugally, while they attend post-secondary institutions for one year. For that same amount of money almost 4,000 students could live for four years as they work towards an honours degree. And how about the almost 42,000 that this Bernston fella stole from the province? That would finance eight students through to honours degrees. After that, they would be assets to the province's economy if they live and work here. Oh stop, I say to myself, you just get upset with this kind of consideration.

Perhaps it would be appropriate to consider education through the eyes and understanding of some of our ancestors: From "The Soul of an Indian," the words of Charles Alexander Eastman, or Ohiyesa, "We taught our children by both example and instruction, but with emphasis on example... we considered the fundamentals of education to be love of the Great Mystery, love of nature, and love of people and country."

Tatanga Mani, a Stoney Indian said "The Great Spirit has provided you and me with the opportunity for study in nature's university, the forests, the rivers, the mountains and the animals which included us."

From his centennial soliloquy, Chief Dan George, "... I shall rise again out of the sea; I shall grab the instruments of the white man's success – his education, his skills, and with these new tools I shall build my race into the proudest segment of your society... I shall see our young braves and our chiefs sitting in the houses of law and government, ruling and being ruled by the knowledge and freedom of our great land."

Were these wise people sages, philosophers, prophets, teachers or just idealists? Perhaps they were all of that and more. When

I consider what they thought and taught, I can only arrive at the conclusion that if their teachings became my living, there is a power to be reckoned with. After all, one of the greatest powers we know has been identified as knowledge. All of life is learning and all of us can learn.

Bernelda Wheeler

The Souls Inside of Them

And the wind howls in the deserts
And the wind moans the songs of their souls
Songs of the worlds inside of them
Songs of their pain and their shame
And the songs escape in search of expression
And they fight and they kill and they maim
And death comes and parents weep in their grief
And we know where the fury was born
But it lives in the deserts within their souls
The souls inside of them

And the wind howled in the desert
And the wind moaned the song of her soul
The song of the world inside of her
The Song that was locked – imprisoned within
The song that sobbed in her pain and her shame
The song that held secrets it gave to the desert
And the desert sand was cold
And the desert enslaved her in solitude
That desert within her soul
The soul inside of her

And the wind howled in the desert
And moaned the turbulent song of her soul
As she lay with her face in the sand
And the desert sand was cold
And the images floated around her
Haunted her shape shifting self
The face of a holy man – trusted by all
Her escape was only a dream but she ran
To the desert within her soul
The soul inside of her

Bernelda Wheeler

Still the wind howled in the desert
And relentlessly sobbed the song of her soul
It told her to rise, to run and to shout
Expose the face of the one who preyed
The one who wore robes, the one who prayed
The one who preyed, who preyed and preyed
On a helpless child too frail to resist
All the pain all the shame of the brutal acts
So she hides in the desert within her soul
The soul inside of her

So the wind howls in the desert
And the wind moans this song of her soul
For years it has howled: it has moaned the story
Of hypocrisy wrapped in the robes of the church
While the victim survives in shuddering shame
Of acts she was told were hers to keep
To keep from the world – to keep to herself
The acts became thoughts and memories boiled
They hide in the desert within her soul
The soul inside of her

And the wind is in turmoil and howls to be free
And it moans the agonized songs of souls
It whips around corners and slashes at shadows
Seeking a way to a world that is clean
Seeking to scatter in fragments the fetid thoughts of souls
The ones that are locked – imprisoned in hate
In fear of the robes and rosary power
The power that perpetrates pain
The pain that hides in the deserts of souls
The Souls inside of them

And the wind howled and roared and tore
And it wailed the songs of their souls

Bernelda Wheeler

And it cursed the robes and rosary power
That tore at the flesh of its children
And the rage of the wind found a crack in the desert
And it thrashed at the pain and the shame
Until they slithered through cracks in the sand
And left the deserts within those souls
The souls inside of them

And the stillness was strange when no wind howled
No wind moaned the songs of their souls
And the desert was bare – the images gone
And they rose from the floor of the desert
And the desert sand was warm
And the wind was alive and whispered songs
And the breeze caressed their thoughts
Then life came back – lush life to the land
To the deserts within their souls
The souls inside of them

But the wind still howls in the deserts
And it moans the songs of other souls
And the deserts are bare and bleak
But the images come in their slithering slime
Come to torment, to tear and to tease
Come in their robes and their habits
To torture to damn – to hate in contempt
While they kneel at the alters of prayer
And the wind waits in the deserts
The deserts in other souls
The souls inside of them

And the Pope prays
And the Priest preys
And the nun babbles beads of the rosary

Metamorphosis

Bernelda Wheeler

Requiem for a Country Daughter

She was a daughter of her beloved Canada.
From the earth she dug seneca root.
From the trees and plants she picked berries,
And in the forest she hunted rabbit, partridge
prairie chicken and deer.
She fed the earth with seeds
And nurtured them to food, for her family.
She cried and prayed for her loved ones
Through two world wars.
A mother of many children,
her midwife skills welcomed over 365 children to the world
And her healing hands helped scores back to health.
Who knows how many have walked in the moccasins she made,
Have been protected by the vests and jackets
Fashioned by her hands,
Have appreciated the beadwork of her design.
She made the best damn pork and beans we ever had
And fed them to us on bowling nights.
Her greatest source of pride was in her Aboriginal roots
But the Scotsman in the woodpile
Emerged in her anger and excitement
And she shouted her rage in Scottish brogue.
A fearless four foot-ten,
She stomped and cried, prayed and worked,
Loved and taught her way through 89 years of life
And dragged us behind her.
But her eyes grew dim; her strength grew less
And she waited to meet her beloved Colin and their three sons.
The wait is over. She's with our dad
And relatives long gone
And probably met them clutching her sweetgrass.
To all her descendants, relatives and friends,
She leaves a legacy of strength, determination, spunk

Bernelda Wheeler

Pride and overwhelming love.
Have a pleasant journey Mom,
And don't you worry,
Pastor Fox gonna pray real hard for your soul.
Take our love.
See you in the next world
All your kids, relations, students and friends.

Bradlee LaRocque

Failing Peyote 101

Peyote colours my vision.
I close my eyes, set
My chin onto my knees
And see fire dance like prairie grass.

Falling deeply,
Water drum massaging my flesh away.
I lean heavily into rattles' voice
And climb up into
the belly of an eagle.

Flying backward in time.
Landscape in negative,
No highways or bridges,
I drop out over the valley before I go too far.

My body falling heavily.
Pop my head up before I hit the ground.
Road man smiles, elbows Harry
And says, "He was gone."

Water bird prays at sunrise,
Feeds me Corn, Berries and Tongue Soup.
Dreaming of my eagle
"Good Mornings" warm my hands.

Duane Niatum

The Story of Our Name

"Grandfather, you promised us a story if we sat still for ten seconds. I bet we've been still for one giant minute, Grandpa! We also watched our guardian, the Sun, travel down its sky path. And that took another minute.

Yes, Grandpa, we never said a word as the Sun traveled through our village and on into the waves and spray. And for another story, Grandma promised she would help me bake a huckleberry pie you won't forget! It's an old family secret, Grandpa. And sweetness is its name! So, with this gift waiting to surprise, can I ask you for one that maybe your grandfather told you? Chipmunk says your lodge is made of stories, grandpa. And you once told me at bedtime that the night is a lake of stories and as endless and deep as the pathway of stars."

"Ah, my little agate eye and my little maiden-hair ferns. There's a story I can tell you that my grandfather told me when I was a boy about your age. It was so long ago I need a medicine paddle to get back to that beach as white as the belly of our very distant and flat-eyed cousin, the flounder.

Many, many sun and moon cycles ago, a great Chief, from a village near the coastal cliffs, decided he would have a Potlatch to celebrate his long life and the good health and prosperity of his growing family. He sent runners in four directions to invite all the neighbouring villages and other tribes to attend his feast. He had spent autumn, winter, and spring in preparation, and he was in the mood to welcome guests and have a little fun. There was a rich harvest of food that had been gathered by his family, and gifts created for the honoured guests he expected from as far away as the feast bird could fly and announce the occasion of the raising of a new Longhouse.

The Chief wanted everyone to know that the sea had offered the best dishes known to exist for this feast, and the forest had things to offer too. He was confident that no one would leave for his or her village feeling hungry or disappointed.

Nothing had been left out of his plan. Even Thunderbird, whose voice was made of mountains, had given a flash of approval. And a daughter had sewn him a new cedar vest for the event. With such love, how could anything go wrong?

The dancing would begin as soon as the Welcome Song was over and who knows how many dawns would pass before the feasting and dancing would stop. His orator's staff would shine like a cranberry in sunlight. He could feel in his heart the blood of his people would course through their veins like their sacred river.

The Chief had made sure that the young people that attended would have many games to play. And my little ones, you too would have had fun attending this feast. And the parents and grandparents were promised the bone game to play. Drums would be placed into position and singers would be formed for both sides. No one would be left out of the play circle.

Tribes came from up and down the coast in their great sea canoes and those now lined the beach for more than a hundred yards. The Chief had asked his guests to come and join him in putting the finishing touches on a Longhouse he and his family had built. He said this ceremonial Longhouse was a gift to his people and all his family members coming from neighbouring villages. He told his guests of all the events that were to take place during the festival and pointed out that the special event would be the placing of the center log on the top of the newly built smokehouse. The event was a contest and the Chief wanted to discover which tribe could raise the log in to position. Therefore, each village Chief was asked to have his men approach and give it a try.

A few tribes could not even lift the log off the ground. Other villagers could barely get it off the ground and were unable to lift it up to their shoulders. No matter how hard they tried; none of the men could raise the log above their heads. Tribe after tribe stepped forward and could not get the log into position. You could see the sweat drop from their faces like rain.

It was then time for our ancestors to give it a try. As the men approached the log they started singing an old, old song. Each man in the family raised an arm to honour the path of the Sun making its way beyond the village and far out into the white-mouthed sea. Our men could hear snickers and chuckles from a few of the men from visiting tribes. Our women and children also heard how poor the other tribes' manners had become. But your ancestors kept to the rhythm and pace of the song and the dance toward the log. And by standing within the full basket of their song, they were able to ignore the laughing and catcalls of the bad-mannered guests. It is true that we are not considered a people tall in stature. Nevertheless, we have never been known for our weak natures or flat-footed songs. Many tribes up and down this coast have honoured our singers. Still, some of the taller people from neighbouring tribes looked as if they were thinking to themselves: 'If we couldn't lift that heavy log over our shoulders and drop it in to place, how can the Klallams think they can? They are almost as short as the Little People of the forest; anyone can see they are going to make fools of themselves.'

As our men approached the log, they could feel the blood of the earth move up through their legs and spine to their shoulders. So their power song told them that the log would be theirs. The men expected to do it and they did. Our leader called the men together and had them stand on one side of the log instead of some of them on each side. The hosts and those from other villages watched every step our ancestors took and appeared to laugh to themselves and say under their breaths, "What do these foolish people think they are up to? Are they begging us to laugh at them? Do they think we want to act as silly as them?"

After our leader whispered to the men what they were going to do, they began to roll the log. The men could hear almost everyone else laugh as they moved the log. Our men sang their power song and ignored the strangers' loud laughter and blue jay squawks. They remained steady and focused in their every move and action. They shut out any distraction from their goal. Our men had watched carefully and closely the methods of the other tribes and they had formulated their own strategy. In council they chose a path and their determination could be heard in the song.

Their wives and children acted as a chorus of support as the men rolled the log down to the water and floated it out until it was even with their shoulders. Our men hoisted it on to their shoulders and waded out of the water; they sang from deep within their inner natures and their eyes focused on the path ahead. They could almost see the earth breathe. Now the people from the other tribes watched in silence and became shy puzzles searching for shadows to hide in. The wives and children of your ancestors sang in waves around the men's chanting. The men stepped over to the Longhouse with the center log firmly on their shoulders. Our leader gave the signal that after the count of three all the men were to heave the log. When the leader called out three, and heave, heave, heave, the Klallam men in unison pushed the big log-pole upward and it fell into place on the top of the Longhouse.

When our ancestors finished their song and turned to honour the host community, the Chief of the Potlatch stepped up to them to distribute many gifts in thanks. They were later honoured with songs and dances by the village host. All the other guests at the feast joined in the singing and dancing. The many fires along this coast thus became for a few seasons one village of peace. From that day to the present, the other tribes around us have called our people, the Klallams, 'the Strong People.'"

"Oh, Grandpa," one of the granddaughters asked, "Is it really a true story? I think it must be true because I suddenly feel stronger than I did yesterday," as she giggled and hid her face inside her mother's shawl.

"Well, little yellow willow, the storyteller says it's an old, old story, and he believes it is true as our lives or the changes of the seasons." Their grandfather then laughed and spoke to his special granddaughter again. "My sweet girl, it's as true as the path of the Sun that comes and goes throughout our lives, whether we welcome it from home or far away. Our Elders from long ago told us as children that the Sun could easily be your oldest grandfather on this green ball of mountain, forest, and sea. Only Raven might be older, especially the slippery side of his shadow. And did you feel how the Sun shined a little brighter when the log fell into place at the top of the longhouse?"

The girls' faces shined like crabapples with the joy of story and family and quickly answered, "Yes, Grandpa, Oh, yes!"

AFTERWORD

The inspiration for writing this adaptation of a Klallam sacred narrative was to lend support to the Klallams at Lower Elwha, Jamestown, and Port Gamble who are encouraging the young people to learn the language, songs, and stories of their ancestors. I hope the modern context for the story will help draw them into its world. Furthermore, key figures in the narrative are also youths, and this too, should appeal to their interest. We have passed the point where we can ignore the fact that the Klallam language is endangered, and with it our oral traditions. For decades even before I was born, the forces of Euroamerican culture, particularly those of the missionaries, federal government and non-Native educators, succeeded in convincing or shaming American Indian children and youth into ignoring or resisting all aspects of their tribal heritage. The Language Preservation Center at Lower Elwha was created several years ago to turn that around.

Blood of the Earth

The last drop of water fell with a tinkle. Maria Blacksmith picked up the battered tin pail and carried it inside. Two copper bowls gleamed on the kitchen countertop. She poured water into them and prayed.

"Grandmother Moon, Grandmothers of the Four Directions, thank you for this day; thank you for the sacred circle of life; thank you for protecting my family and for guiding me toward this sacred day."

Maria was happy her brother wasn't around. Tommy always left the peanut butter jar open, and he never put the bannock away. She had the kitchen all to herself to prepare the food for the feast. A haunch of deer, it's purple-red flesh dark against the gleaming sink, lay in a pool of thick blackening blood. She heaved the leg onto the countertop with a grunt. A smile crept across her face. "I'm entering the Women's Circle tonight," she said for the twentieth time since waking.

Using their sharpest knife, the young Cree girl sawed off two large pieces of meat, put them into a plastic bowl, and took it to the table. Just as she put the rest into the fridge, the phone rang. Maria hesitated a moment before racing to the far wall to pick it up.

"Tansi, Maria here," she said.

It was her cousin Susie. "Hello. What 'cha doing?"

"Hey Cuz. Don't your remember, I'm getting ready for the ceremony tonight. I'm just making the stew. Want to come over and visit while I work?"

A long sigh whistled over the receiver, "Ah gee, I thought we could get together over here for awhile. I just got the new Seventeen magazine," said Susie.

Maria frowned. She had told Susie yesterday that she'd be busy cooking today.

"I've got too much to do. Why don't you come over here?" she asked again.

Although Susie's mother, along with several aunts, belonged to the Women's Circle, she didn't want any part of it.

"Mmm. I don't know," murmured her cousin.

Maria could tell that Susie was already bored. "Why not? We can talk then. We haven't had a good visit in a long time," she said.

"Nah. Hey, is Tommy around? Maybe he can come over. Since I hardly ever see you anymore, we've been kinda' hanging out."

Surprised, Maria asked, "What have you guys been up to?"

Susie said, "I shouldn't be telling you this. The gang'll kill me... but, we've been smoking. You know, pot. It's lots of fun. You should come over. I've got a little bit with me right now. Pete lets us girls take some."

Maria felt a thud in the pit of her stomach. Tommy was only eleven and Susie, at fifteen, was only two years older than she. Pete: probably Pete McKay. He had just moved back to Pine Hills from Winnipeg.

"Susie, I don't like this. Why are you and Tommy getting involved with that stuff. And with that guy?" Maria realized she was shouting.

Lowering her voice, she continued, "Didn't you know Pete was in jail for robbing some old ladies? Old ladies. What kind of person does that?"

Susie sounded annoyed, "Oh Maria, Pete's done his time. He's not hurting anyone. Look, I gotta go. If Tommy shows up, tell him what I said, okay? Okay?"

Maria hung up then switched the ringer off. She thought about going to see her cousin, but a quick look at the clock showed that it was nearly two o'clock. The ceremony was to start at six.

"I'll go see her tomorrow," she thought, and went back to the meat.

Two and a half hours later a delicious aroma filled the house. The stew was bubbling on the stove, and four brown bannock lay stacked on the counter. Bannock was best when cut up just before serving so she left it. A layer of just-rinsed blueberries glistened on the table.

Maria gave the stew a stir and took it off the burner. She took the butter out to soften. Everything looked ready. She took off her apron and was about to leave the kitchen when she suddenly stopped.

"The tea," she screeched.

The older women liked camp tea: tea boiled until it was black as night. Maria found the big teapot in the back of a cupboard, filled it with water and tea bags, and put it on to boil. Then she had just enough time for a shower.

Ten minutes later, Maria raced downstairs, a wet braid slapping the back of a turquoise ribbon shirt. She also wore a long red skirt decorated with two rows of turquoise ribbons. On her feet were new floral beaded moccasins: a present from her father.

The tea was boiling hard so she turned the element down to low. The bannocks were cut into squares and put into a basket. The blueberries would look best in a glass bowl. Utensils, plates and bowls went onto a tray and into the living room. Earlier, the furniture was moved against the walls. A yellow and black rug lay in the center of the room, ready for the feast on one side and the ceremonial altar on the other. After arranging the tray, Maria set the bowls of water out.

A blue suitcase was on the couch. Opening it, she took out a turtle rattle, a smaller painted leather rattle and an eagle wing. These she placed where she and her mother usually sat in the circle. Then, Maria took out two long braids of sweetgrass and a bag of sage; medicine she'd gathered last month. These were set close to the water, along with a copper ashtray and a box of wooden matches. Everything looked perfect. Satisfied, she returned to the kitchen to get the food.

The sound of tires crunching on the gravel driveway announced that someone was home. Would Tommy be with them? Should she tell Mom and Dad? As she agonized, the door opened and her mother called out, "Maria. Are you home?"

"Yeah. I'm in here," she answered.

Ida Blacksmith was a tall woman with fine features. She had on an old green coat flecked with tiny bits of cedar. Maria guessed she'd been at the Sweat Lodge.

"Tommy and Dad stopped off at Uncle Morrie's. They're going to stay there for the evening. Dad said to tell you he'll be thinking about you," she said with a smile.

She took off her coat and carried it to the hall closet, calling out, "I'm glad Tommy's with him. He's been acting kind of funny lately. Just like he doesn't want to be around us anymore."

Maria could hear the worry in her voice. As she was about to blurt out what she knew, her mother appeared in the doorway. "I'm so proud of you, my girl. There are so few girls that come into the Women's Circle. Oh, Maria, tonight is so special for me," she said, hugging her close.

The sharp tang of cedar smelled good. Tonight was supposed to be sacred, a time to celebrate being a woman. How could either of them concentrate if they were worried about Tommy?

Maria looked up, "It's special for me too, Mom," she said quietly. Her mother's bottom lip pulled slightly to the left, the result of a mild stroke last year.

Susie and Tommy's problem could wait one more day.

Gently moving away, her mother said briskly, "We should finish getting ready."

"The food is ready. The ceremony stuff is out. What else should I do?" said Maria.

"Go smudge the living room. I'll bring the food in," she answered.

Maria nodded and left. Kneeling, she picked up a sweetgrass braid and broke the knot off. She lit the pale green plait with a wooden match. Taking the wing, Maria brushed fragrant smoke over the objects on the rug, including the food her mother had just put down. Then, she walked around the room, waving the smoke outward. When she was finished, the door opened. Great-aunt Sophie came in. Maria put the smoldering braid in the ashtray then went over. Her arms easily went around the frail body.

Sophie Panagot was a small, sprightly woman who'd endured seven horrific years at the Thicket Portage Residential School before coming home with a Grade Six diploma. From that day, her Great-aunt, now fifty seven, would only speak in Cree and refused to enter a church. At funerals, she'd wait outside; sometimes, in a howling storm.

"*Tansi, Nitanisin,*" she said.

Maria's smiled and replied, "*Tansi.* It's good to see you Auntie. Let me take your bundle. I'll put it over there."

As she turned with the red woolen bag cradled in her arm, a familiar voice spoke from the door.

"You have been busy. Stew smells good."

Susie. Maria gave her cousin a quick grin. Her mom was putting several large, square cushions down on the floor. For the next half hour, Maria was busy putting away coats and taking bundles so she could only wonder why Susie was there.

At last, old Mrs. Yellowback came in supported by her two granddaughters. She was the head woman of the Pine Hills Women's Circle. The women gently lowered her onto a cushion set against the couch. Soon, soft laughter and women's voices filled the house.

At a raised hand from Mrs. Yellowback, the women began opening bundles and laying out their contents. Maria lit a sage ball and smudged all the items. Then she went to each woman, smudging her. Her mother turned off the lamps and lit a fat green candle; it would represent fire.

Great-aunt Sophie filled the bowls of a dozen carved redstone pipes with tobacco before passing them to their keeper. Each woman cradled her pipe in her left arm, waiting until everyone had their own. Maria took her place on the floor beside her mother, smiling across at Susie. Mrs. Yellowback's pipe was lit. In a singsong voice, the head woman began to pray.

"*Tansi*. My name is Yellow Cloud Woman. I am of the Wolf Clan. I am a Cree woman. Creator of all living things, thank you for the gift of life. Thank you for the gifts you give us each day: the sun, the moon, the stars, the medicines, and all that make our lives good. Thank you Mother Earth. I thank you for the wonderful gift of water: the blood of the earth. Thank you for giving to us women, the responsibility and duty to care for the water."

Each Pipe Carrier silently said her own prayer as Mrs. Yellowback continued. The now-lit pipes were offered to the six sacred directions: upward for the Creator; downward for Mother Earth; then once toward the East, the North, the West; and finally, to the South. After each offering the pipe was turned left in a full circle. Once those honors were done, the women sat back to smoke. A peaceful silence enveloped the room.

When the pipes were finished, her mother whispered, "You do the water ceremony."

Maria rose and walked carefully around the rug. She picked up the copper bowl, raising it while acknowledging Mother Earth for giving the gift of water. A gentle clatter broke out. Her mother, with a slight back and forth movement, sounded the turtle rattle. The small stones inside the dried shell pulsed in a rhythm that seemed to match Maria's own heartbeat: steady and strong. She closed her eyes and spoke the blessing of the water. Finally, Maria spilled a small amount onto the rug, symbolically giving back to Mother Earth what she had taken. Then she took the bowl over to Mrs. Yellowback and offered her the first drink. The old woman's black eyes met hers. Maria felt wonderful. At this very moment, everything was good in her life.

Later, after hand-made gifts of skirts and leather pouches

had been given and admired, and the food eaten with relish, the girls had a few moments to talk as they did the dishes. With arms deep in warm soapy water, Maria asked her cousin why she'd come. Susie was silent for a moment.

"I had a visit from Mrs. Yellowback just after we talked," she began, "And she told me that Pete's her grandson."

Maria's eyes opened wide and turning to Susie with her mouth slightly open, said, "I didn't know that."

"Yeah. Neither did I. Anyway, Pete's had a visit from the R.C.'s. One of the kids got into trouble and told her parents about the," she glanced around, "Ah... about what was going on. Mrs. Yellowback got Pete to tell her all the kid's he's been hanging out with. He must have given up all of us because she came over to see me. Her and Great-aunt Sophie came. Like I said, she talked to me."

Maria shook her head. Relief flowed through her. Her cousin would be okay. Tommy would be all right too. The ceremony had been beautiful. Tonight, the women had welcomed another member into their circle.

"No," Maria thought, looking at her cousin, "Tonight, there were two new members."

Margaret McKay-Sinclair Ruiz

My Memoirs (excerpt)

Spring Catch on the Lower Falls, 1930 – 1931

An event that took place every year was scoop-net fishing at the mighty rapids below the falls. Scoop-net fishing was one of my favorite outings as a youngster. We would all get into rugged clothes after church on a Sunday and start our six-mile hike to the rapids. There would be about thirty or forty middle-aged women, sons and daughters. To me it was a beautiful sight to see the glistening chunks of icicles hanging from the rugged rocks on the noisy falls and a magical sunrise of many different colors that would dodge behind the icy rocks and play tricks on one's eyes. This was nature at it's best. Dad was always the leader and my favorite aunt, Sarah would tell us girls folklore stories and about her younger days as we walked. We all loved to listen. But the boys were always in a hurry to get there and they would tell Dad, "Those girls talk too much." All they wanted was to get there fast to see who could get more fish. We girls were always too slow in finding the best rock to stand on. By the time we arrived at the rapids, our brothers and friends were already scooping fish. Sarah would say, "Watch out, boys, the ladies are just as good as you! They'll maybe even catch you a sturgeon for dinner tonight." The Saskatchewan was very high from the melting snow and this made the river very fast-flowing. But that didn't keep the many fishermen and women from standing on those rugged rocks-we would all try our luck. At the foot of our great roaring rapids, hundreds of large and small pikes, white fish, and sturgeon as well as jackfish and pickerel found their way down the river that was also full of ice, broken branches, and trees. This was quite a sight to watch as we tried to scoop fish for mother's table.

Margaret McKay-Sinclair Ruiz

Fall in Grand Rapids – 1930's

I just now remembered how we all got our moccasins for the long, winter months. Well, fall was the time for great moose hunts. Every man that had a gun went out to their favorite hunting ground to bag their moose meat for winter use. While the men were gone, we women would go for our fall berry picking. The berries were in the high bush; cranberries, moss berries, butter berries. We used to pick by the pail-full so our mothers could prepare them in bulk. The men would always get a moose and would dry and store the meat away for later use. Then the moose hides would be ready for the women to prepare. First they would scrape all the fat from the hides down by the river, wash off all the blood, etc. Then they would put the skin on a rack and leave the skin on this high rack. Later, two or three women would scrape the fur and after this, the other side of the hide, until all matter and fur was gone. It took almost two weeks for this process. Then the hide was put on another rack to hang there to dry for one week. Then the women would use a sharp knife made of stone. They would scrape like heck to make the huge moose hide as soft as velvet. This was the way to get the hide ready for moccasins for winter wear. After this step, they would again hang the hide on a high rack above a hole in the ground and would light a fire there with rotten tree stumps. This was to tan the hide to a lovely brown or a golden tan color. It took the women four days to tan a large hide. The smoke from the old tree stumps and trees lasted all day. It was a great smoke coming from that hole in the ground. I used to help grandma, but I didn't like how your eyes would get sore from the smoke and turn red. This was the last step. They would do about fifty hides, sometimes more as they made beaded jackets out of them too.

Winter in Grand Rapids

Winter nights were long and this was moccasin-making time with beadwork or silk. Porcupine quills were also used to decorate jackets, muckluks and moccasins. They were all done very pretty especially for women. The women would try to beat each other; who did the best embroidery and beadwork. I used to watch them working hard, sewing beads under kerosene lamps or just plain oil lamps on cold winter nights. The women gathered in a huge hall and made a party out of it. And how they would gossip. I'd listen in at times. Afterward it was so good to wear our fancy moccasins at the New Year's dance or when going to church on Sunday. We loved to show them off. The young men would also show off the fancy beadwork and fringes on their jackets and muckluks. They looked so very handsome. They were all so tall and slim. Even though things were real primitive in those days compared to now, I am thankful for the way I was brought up. I was lucky to live in a time when folks could live off the land on God-given talents and skills.

Janet Duncan

unchartered territory

Strange and scary sites
on these unfamiliar grounds
what laws apply here? I ask myself
and feel that somehow I am
needlessly stepping over and around obstacles
that stand in the way of an otherwise clear path

My idea of peaceful cheeriness
Don't I enjoy steep hills?
The climb the oxygen the sweat
the downhill swiftness
A challenge where once climbed is
no longer a strain but a memory...
With an acknowledged new strength
and higher vision...
vision, I think I am lacking that now

Yes steep hills are fine
in their own
I prefer to use the ridges
and climb from slope to slope
with the sense of the wilderness
around me
Pathways to comfort and sustenance
without disturbing the natural
balance
It is here where I am able to
see clearly the threat of
boundaries being broken by
another's footprint
or by my own

Janet Duncan

An individual or
shared space where a
sacred ground has been
trodden on by either
disrespect or truth
Both are felt the impact
and hackles raised are
slow to relax while the
scent stays fresh and the
minds eye alert
for territorial sign
Scratching and digging
and rubbing and rooting
in mud holes, trails,
trees and stone
water holes shared by
one after another
in groups or solitude
the understanding is the same
the signs are there
and each one creature
marks the trail with their
presence replaced or accepted
by members of the wilderness freeway

It is my presence and survival
that I seek to defend
acknowledgement and respect
in honouring myself I say
I say... I say... I say...
respect and honour and acknowledgement!
I tromp through the day
stamping each foot again and again
to emphasize the point
Who's spirit is stronger?

Janet Duncan

The loud thundering of grouse's wing beat
or the soft continuous singsong of chickadee
Survival of the fittest
indeed
The elements are flurried and cold
or scorching and dry
and who admits defeat, not I
no
in great effort I turn the
rotting stump and dig
nibbling sweet morsels at my leisure and right
hmmph!
hmmph!

Donald Blais

Timely License
Deliberately
Circumnavigated

Nick
Black Elk, a one time
Lakota Shaman
taught "*Wakan-Tanka...*
Everything
comes from Him,
and... everything
returns to Him."[1]
The cycle of
cosmic salvation.

Have you ever noticed that
Creator doesn't seem
to get bored
making one human
being
after another,
snowflake after snowflake,
grain of sand after grain of sand,
and each just
slightly
different enough
as if an adolescent prank?
Is it because
Creator enters upon
His-Her activity
with the attitude of
playfulness? The
sun rises, the
sun sets, and

Donald Blais

The end is the beginning,
the beginning is the end
with no twin between them. A
dream catcher, a
medicine wheel, the
sacred hoop, the
circle of life.
Paper doll after
paper doll after
paper doll.
Yo-yos,
pinwheels,
frisbees and
slinkies:
cyclical motion.
Spinning,
spinning
yarns and
threads of
timelessness, and
dreams, and
hope.

Cyclical playfulness is
elemental to the whole
plan of
cosmic salvation: it is the
woof and whistle and the
archetype from which
everything has its purpose. It is in
play that
people and
things
become whole.

Donald Blais

A slapstick comedy of
divine proportions,
elking round the bend
in the
Nick of
time.

FOOTNOTE

1. Nicholas Black Elk with Joseph Epes Brown, The Sacred Pipe (Norman, OK: University of Oklahoma Press, [1953] 1989), p. 80.

Karen Coody Cooper

As The Prow Cuts Through Water

for Jim

He shaped the steamed wood
Into pieces for a vessel
That would carry them back
To familiar headwaters.

He shaped the young boy
Into a vessel
Who would move forward through
The arduous currents of time.

There is never silence in the woods,
The grandfather said,
For even silence is a sound.
You're never alone outside, he said,
There are always ears listening
And you may as well learn to talk to them.

He made the child bathe in winter streams
Which taught the boy to curse
But such a grandfather as walks on the surface of snow
Is a tangible saviour (and fine craftsman of snowshoes).

While weather-hardened hands
Shaved gunwales to hard satin
And split to their thinnest possibility,
The young boy watched
And patterned himself in
The image of his grandfather.

As the prow cuts through water,
Ripples become the journey's record of memory

Karen Coody Cooper

And while following those ahead of you,
You make your own ripples.
And yours join theirs.

In a canoe you face forward
Toward the things you follow.
When the boy became a grandparent
He still followed the grandfather before him.

Fran Pawis

For The Children

I had a dream

The children needed me

The only answer it would seem

Was becoming a teacher, it had to be.

The long hours were hard

My labour of love

It will show on the card

Yes a teacher, with help – from above.

At Queens, I've left my handprint

Go look – its been left there

What a hard stint

It will show that – I care.

The children inspire me

I've shown them the way

They'll do it too – you'll see

It's meant to be – I say.

Fran Pawis

Inspiration Encourages Transformation

The Ministry of Education

has granted me credit before

I've never failed, so far

I've never tried so hard.

I love working with children

They give me great joy

I'm seeking my ultimate goal

My Ontario Teacher's Certificate

my Aboriginal Teacher Education diploma.

My time spent teaching children

I saw their spirits advance and grow

The inspiration encourages transformation

which will lead them to their ultimate goal.

Fran Pawis

Soon

A long hard struggle
Is almost over
The end is almost in sight
My dream will soon become reality.

I'll be that teacher
My dreams come true
It's not quite over
But soon – very soon.

I did it for the children
I love teaching them
They are so very special
We'll be together again, soon.

I did it the hard way
My example should shine
All you need is a dream
Believe in yourself – follow that dream!

I searched for my dream
My desire was strong
I never gave up
Even at the darkest hour.

Many, many times, I doubted
I shed many tears
There was no way I could quit
Because of dear friends and the Creator

– I survived.

Fran Pawis

Allow yourself to dream
Reach out – dare to try
Grab onto that impossible goal
Your dreams can come true.

April Severin

Testimony

As a tadpole I could only tread water.
As a frog I swim in the present,
burrow into the past,
leap toward the future,
call out to you,
    again and again.
Will you hear me now?

Shirley Brozzo

My People Paid

In 1492
Columbus sailed the ocean blue
Wind filled the sails
Maps were askew
He thought he'd found India
Named us anew

And my people
Paid
With our blood

In 1607
Jamestown was born
Colonists were starving
Powhatan gave them some corn
They survived
They thrived
No longer to mourn

And my people
Paid
With our honour

Louisiana Purchase
Treks to the west
Further they pushed us
Further removed
Taking the land that was best
Pushed us and moved us
Moved us and pushed
Towards the ocean
The mountains
The badlands
And just

Shirley Brozzo

My people
Paid
With our land

Hollywood images
Mascots galore
Whopping
Face painting
Dancing on gym floors
Took our self-esteem
Self-worth
Pride
And more

And my people
Paid
With our self-respect

It's 2001
Time for change is here
Stand up and speak
Raise a voice
Strong and clear
Our religion
Culture
Language
Now strong
Time for change
Is here

As my people
Reclaim
our lives.

Shirley Brozzo

Misshepeshu

On some days when the sky above is clear and filled with sunshine, or coated in fleeting white clouds, he takes life slowly. At times there is barely a ripple to disturb his calmness. It is the type of day that fishermen rejoice in and the freighters are commanded to go "full steam ahead." Beneath the waters aquatic creatures frolic and play, basking in serenity. Along populated shores swimmers delight in the calmness and venture into his cool confines. People seeking their pleasure with a picnic basket or a beach blanket for sunning themselves flock to his banks. Individuals with children or with dogs walk along the beachfront, playing in the calm waters, building sand castles, or throwing rocks or sticks into his great expanse. Writers or people who are stressed wander along his shores seeking solace in the gentle movements of the water. Meanwhile, desolate areas are caressed as he ebbs and flows as a part of his life, much like we breathe in and out without having to think about it. But don't let *Misshepeshu* fool you. He can change his attitude without warning.

Like a man taken in by the bottle, his demeanor changes, often without warning. His waters begin churning and bubbling. A once calm exterior is replaced with waves large enough to scare off small water crafts and make freighter pilots pay attention to the paths before them. The fish people and others who live in *Misshepeshu's* world head for nooks and crannies, the hiding places within his confines, only venturing out for a quick bite to eat, then darting back into hiding again. Near the cities there are still people who congregate along the shore. Some are thrilled at the idea of being able to surf on the greatest of lakes. These people taunt *Misshepeshu* by surfing or trying to swim, not realizing the power he has, creating swiftly moving underwater currents, undertows and whirlpools. The winged people have trouble staying afloat or diving for food and quickly return to the sky, a sky which even reflects

Misshepeshu's mood by turning ugly grey, cloudy, and often blustery. Individuals choosing to walk his shores are often bundled up, still seeking refuge from their reality. Gentle caresses along barren shores become angry slaps as he unleashes his fury. There is very little that can be done to appease him then, with one exception.

All too often when *Misshepeshu* gets like this he claims the lives and souls of those who do not understand his greatness, his power, his strength. Those who do not understand or respect his omnipotence and provoke him by venturing into his domain when he is like this find themselves caught up in his vicelike grip, from which there is often no escape. He has claimed fishermen, swimmers, and sightseerers who did not understand.

He demands reverence. He demands respect. For when he doesn't receive them and his fury turns to rage, like the uncontrollable alcoholic, he doesn't care what happens. Together with the spirit of the sky he conjures up the worst conditions imaginable. Black clouds reflect his disposition. Gale force winds fly across his great expanse as colossal waves rise up to join them. A single soul is not enough to placate this spirit so he reaches out for freighters full, like the Edmund Fitzgerald. The word of the day for the fish people is "dive, dive, dive" as they all head for the depths, to try to escape. Foolhardy people assemble near breakwalls or bridges to marvel at his magnificence but sometimes forget that although a single soul may not feed his hunger, it is a start. Too many forget to honour him, and lose their lives. In punishment he gobbles up lakeshore cabins, homes or small boats until he exacts his dues. Uninhabited areas fare no better as he pummels shorelines, swallowing trees, then spits them out miles away. His tirade may last for an hour or for days, until he feels appeased. He can be the most docile of creatures, if people would remember to respect him. But since we are humans, and tend to forget, he will continue taking revenge soul by soul.

Gordon de Frane

Oldest Medicine In the World

I recall a story Johnny Moses told once. His story was about rock medicine, the oldest medicine in the world. He said it was the oldest medicine in the world and I believed him. "Rock medicine has been around since time immemorial," he said. Rock medicine is powerful, so very powerful indeed.

I used to wonder though; I've never heard a rock speak, not ever. I used to wonder, could it mean that rocks can't speak or that they just choose not to speak?

I know that plants speak to us! Oh, I know they don't speak like human peoples do; at least that's what the *xunitum* believe; but speak they do nevertheless. I know they speak; all I have to do is watch their words as they talk with me. The language they use is in the colour, shape, and growth that whisper quietly to me. They tell me when it's blossom season by flushing with new green shoots and buds. They tell me when it's time to harvest when they send up the first new growth of spring. Of course, what the Hungry People don't know is that Plant Peoples do talk the way we do. Plants also tell me when it's almost summertime, when the sockeye return. They do this by enticing me with berries. Plants also tell me when they are not happy; they tell me when they need water, or when they are sick. I can tell this by watching the leaves wilt, change colour sometimes they die.

Plant People also tell me when autumn is coming; their leaves change from vibrant green to gold, to crimson, to amber and finally to russet. They drop their leaves rather then risk being damaged by the transforming winds of the winter moons. Through the brilliant colours they wear at this time, they whisper to me: prepare for winter.

I remember as a child hearing laughter and frolicking voices on all sides of me as I walked through the bush, following my dad. He was hunting deer while I was hunting other things: milky quartz, interesting plants and pinecones fallen from the pines and firs above. We had gotten separated. I was so intent on finding treasures and gifts of interest that I just lost sight of him. Later I would find him easily enough as I followed the sound of his rifle bagging the first deer of the season.

It was during that short time apart I became aware of the voices and laughter that seemed to come from everywhere and yet nowhere. I stopped dead in my tracks when I realized what it was and what it meant. I had stumbled into a grove of devil's club. The voices and laughter was coming from the sharp thorny plants that towered over me. But I was in the centre of these potentially pain-inflicting plants I didn't receive so much as a scratch. They were gentle with me and careful not to injure me as I moved about with them. They indulged me like loving grandparents do. I must have been with them for about an hour until I heard the rifle ring out loud. I learned that day that they had recognized me as a relative and were glad that I had stopped to play with them. The memory of that day has stayed with me ever since. Too, since that day, I discovered the medicine of Devil's Club is closely associated with people like me.

People like me are considered special. The plants associated with my kind are sacred too. People like me can whither and die just as plants can wilther and die from lack of sun and water People like me can die from lack of care and love, or because of hate and prejudice. While plants and people drink. I've never seen a rock drink. I've never seen a rock wilt, and I don't think they ever die. But do they speak? That's what I want to know. I also wonder what it was like for our Plant People cousins and other relatives to learn the unfamiliar talk of the Hungry People? What's it like for them to stumble and trip over those foreign words? What's it like for them to hear us offer prayers in that foreign language?

I know Plant People enjoy making our sad and withering hearts happy again. My Elders have taught this to me. They've said that whenever I'm heavy-hearted I should go for a walk in the company of big trees or in a thicket. The people there will lift from me my burden and heal the heaviness that hinders my songs. Indeed, this is very true of big trees. I think taking our sorrow from us makes them even bigger. And I have seen some pretty big trees in my time.

In the sweat, the ribs of the lodge are made from willow who have willingly given-up their lives. They have done this so that those who gather inside can get cleaned. While sitting in the sweat, I listen to the prayers and acknowledgments the *Sch'nem* (one who works with the medicines) as he or shealways give thanks for willows sacrifice. Also inside, in memory of the first darkness, rocks are called the grandfathers. They heat the sweat and impart their medicine to us inside that dark moist home of first homes. Inside, I sing or cry my pain.

Sometimes I see things in the sweat; sometimes, the rocks appear not as rocks but as other people, other things. Each has a story to tell and I listen with ears that cannot hear; I see things with eyes that cannot see. I feel things that cannot be felt. I taste things that cannot be tasted. And I smell things that cannot be smelled.

In the sweat, I've never heard the grandfathers speak. Inside, I hear the prayers and songs offered up in joy and pain, celebration and thanksgiving. The grandfathers gathered in the centre sit quietly as they listen to those of us who speak or sing our pain, letting go of our hurts and offering thanks. They glow crimson in the centre of our world as we sit waiting for their healing medicines to touch us, transform us. They make us shine crimson and our skin grows slick with their medicine working to clean our spirits, making our hearts and minds strong.

The water poured on the grandfathers sings and whistles; still, they remain silent. In their silence I listen for their wisdom, the teachings that will help me and guide me. They stay silent. They hold their tongues, but they witness. And they remember. I learn through their teachings of silence.

I'm reminded of another story about the oldest medicine

in the world. It is a song of prophecy called the Butterfly Song. It tells us that long ago, the rocks thought they were people. I wonder if they talked then, back then when only they existed and humans had not yet fallen from the skies.

When stacked, as in the far north, I wonder, do the rocks speak? When piled, their message tells other people that someone else has been that way. Does this mean they talk like we do?

When painted or etched do rocks speak? Or is it the painted images that speak to those who know and understand. Often, I have seen the *xunitum* buy such painted rocks without so much as a thought. Spirituality cannot be bought or sold. To them even spirit is to be bought and sold.

I think that rocks are very forgiving and accepting of their fates at the hands of those who use them as such. I don't think I would care to be heated to red-hot or scarred with etchings, painted with designs that make me speak when I don't want to. No, it seems rocks are made of much sterner stuff then we humans—the two-legged.

It seems that animals speak, too, but not in our way. The whales sing their songs, sing their words; that's how it was long ago when our storytellers sang the stories. The Seal People bark their words. The Bird People sing and chirp their songs as well. I once heard Johnny Moses sing the Bumblebee Song. And if I close my eyes and think real hard I can recall bits and snippets of the words that the bumblebee sings. Warm and sweet-tasting, the words are like the honey and nectar gathered from the many flowers Bumblebee makes love to.

I've never heard a rock sing. Would its words, its songs, be cold and hard? Or would they sing and whistle like the water that is poured on them in the sweat?

I recall a story about the buffalo and how they came into being on the Great Plains long ago. There was a trickster involved in that story; tricksters are always getting into trouble, it seems. They get into trouble even when they are trying to do good. Many a two-legged has been in such trouble, especially those who govern us, so it seems. And so, the story goes that this trickster fellow was in flight from some failed venture and as he ran he picked up stones along the way throwing them over his shoulder. When each stone touched the earth again it was transformed into the mountains now called The Rockies and among the plains they became the buffalo. Of course, there are no more buffalo on the Great Plains, not like before, anyway. The story also says that even now, the Great Stones, which I've seen on the plains, are the spirits of the buffalo waiting to return one-day. When they return I wonder if we will be here to greet them, to welcome them?

    I wonder what those stones thought as they were being transformed? What is it like to be a mountain? Would the transformed rocks on the plains be pleased to be buffalo again? Would they be pleased to know that they were wiped out last century when the Hungry Ones first appeared? I wonder if they talk amongst themselves as they sit on the Great Plains waiting for another Great Transformation so that they can feed the people once more?

    Each summer when I walk the streets of the land called Windy Place – Victoria – I feel the rock medicine beneath me, imprisoned in the concrete and asphalt covering the earth. They are great black and gray ribbons stretching to the four doorways. These rocks speak when they grow hot beneath the sun's unrelenting smile. Oh, I know they no longer look like rocks, ground, mashed and mixed into *xunitum* stones, but still they are there. And still they remain silent. I think that rocks must be a very forgiving people. I doubt I would stay silent for long if it was me or my relatives ground into concrete or spread like molasses in ribbons across the land.

    Sometimes, I see rocks fit into place, holding up grand houses that the privileged Hungry Ones live in. But only a few of the Hungry Ones live in these places. There are many more Hungry Ones who don't live in such fine homes. Like many of my cousins they live without. For these other Hungry Ones their homes are among the *xunitum* rocks called streets. Their pillows are made of stone. I wonder if the people who live there can hear the rocks speak beneath them? Or have the mouths of the Rock People been ground into silence, forever and ever? Silent again, rocks don't speak, can't with no mouth.

Maybe that's it! Maybe rocks have had their mouths removed. In a way I guess they have.

In Johnny Moses' first story about rocks, he told us his granny had used the medicine in a way that saved her and her grandson, Johnny, from the evils of a heart that could not, would not allow itself to hear their hearts singing to him. Their hearts sang in the language of humans; his heart could not, would not allow this.

The second story is one of hope that the rocks will come back one day and be among the people as the spirit of the buffalo. Rocks it seems can be many things to our people. But still, I have not heard of one speaking!

My cousin William George wrote a poem about Rocks once. His professors failed to understand what it meant. "We are Rock" is one of his lines; we have been here since we first fell from the skies. Still they didn't understand or maybe they didn't want to understand. They failed to understand the medicine of my cousin's words. After all, it's the Hungry People that sell our medicines; that's bad. But what's worse is when one of our own sells it. I figure at least the *xunitum* don't know any better. And we, we who should, have no excuse.

Maybe it's only the Hungry People who cannot hear the rocks speak. This could explain why I couldn't hear them: I'm only a half-breed. Still, I hear other things speak; I see other things speak to me. So maybe I'm not so half-breed after all.

According to Johnny Moses, Rock medicine is the oldest medicine in the world. The Rocks were here before the two-legged fell from the skies. They will be here after the two-legged are gone. Maybe the two-legged had better learn to hear the Rock people before it's too late. And so the Butterfly Song is a prophecy of this time. Maybe Rocks don't talk because we don't know how to listen. That, it seems, is why Rocks choose not to talk. The Hungry People have not the ears to hear them with.

Eric A. Ostrowidzki

YO, Brown-skinned Girls
Don't Steal Gold Rolexes

To Kleya Forté-Escamilla and Gloria Anzaldúa

"Juanita! Juanita-Conseulla Martinez!
Your brother Paco was over here
Looking for you! Him and his homies
Were driving the lipstick-red Mustang–
The one with the bitching black stripes!
He said he don't want you runnin' round
By yourself in the 'hood' no more.
He said it ain't safe for you cuz
There's a drug war goin' on in the *barrio*.
Already too many of Paco's homeboys
Have had their *cajonés* shot off.
Juanita! Are you listening to me?!!
Take off that Walkman and maybe you
Can hear me for a change, baby-sister.
Juanita! Where are you goin' with your
Purple beret and your Sony Walkman?
I'm goin' to tell Paco if you don't listen!"

Everyday Juanita-Conseulla Martinez
Would walk to work at The Tequila Sunrise Motel
Where she made about $3.25 per hour
Changing the linen, making the beds,
Swabbing toilets, sweeping carpets,
Emptying ashtrays, throwing out booze
Bottles and beer cans and condoms, wrapping spotless
Waterglasses in germ-proof tissue; and
Don't Forget to Leave the "House Courtesy Mints"
Upon the pillows. If Juanita was having an especially unlucky day,
One of the male residents would return
To his room before Juanita had a chance

Eric A. Ostrowidzki

To restock the rolls of toilet paper, and,
Flashing a green wad like a Mister Bigbucks from Madrid,
He would lunge at this Chicana girl around
The pinewood doublebed like a blindfolded
Drunkard trying to jab a long wooden pole
At a festive-coloured *papiér mâche* burrow.

With her purple beret worn at
A dangerous slant to the side and her long
Black hair dyed a brilliant parrot-green,
Juanita-Conseulla Martinez always walked
To The Tequila Sunrise each morning.
By 7:00 AM Juanita was sending her
Seven younger brothers off to school,
And by 9:00 AM she was all dressed
In her starched bubblegum-pink uniform
With her Sony Walkman jacked all the way
Up to the goldenflower barrio-moon ready
To give her a boost like no crack-cocaine could
Ever give. Sometimes Juanita-Conseulla
Would turn the volume of her Sony Walkman
Even louder as if to deaf out the
Moans
                And groans
                                  And drones
Of a million lonely whitemen who haunted
The rooms like bleating flannel-gray ghosts.
O sweet Juanita with the blue-black eyes
Like the Homegirl of the Virgin Guadalupe!

She was a $3.25-an-hour-slave,
And her mother was a $1.25-a-day-slave before her,
And her mother's mother was a 50¢-a-week-slave before her.
While she changed the snot-yellow sheets
Of the pinewood doublebeds, picking up

Eric A. Ostrowidzki

A pair of red polka-dotted boxer shorts
And waving them around as if they were

Custer the Clown's Flag of Surrender,

Juanita imagined that she was living
Some other life, in some other place,
Where no Brown-Skinned Girls had
To slave in a Pink Polyester Uniform of Death.
Listening to some righteous blackman rap
About Drugs and Drivebys and Doomsday,
Juanita-Conseulla did not hear
The metallic scratch of a worn key
In the brass cylinder of the doorlock,
Nor did she see the little bald waddling man
In the brown baggy suit enter the room,
Eyeing her with the perverse glee
Of a paedophile in a kindergarten classroom.

Juanita-Conseulla Martinez – Paco's
Younger sister – didn't mean to kill the
Florid portly little Watch-Salesman but when
He started to accuse her of stealing
One of his GOLD ROLEX WATCHES and
Threatened to call the cops if she didn't
Pet his penis as a 'gesture of international goodwill'
Between two hostile nations, Juanita
Panicked, pushing the little whiteman
Down, pushing him hard, hard enough
For him to fall and crack his rosy bald-pate
Against the sharp edge of a glass-topped
Coffee table, with a final, branch-snapping crack.
Out cold. Most likely dead. With his
Tongue lolling out like a dead calf's
Blue tongue engorged in a butcher-shop window.

Eric A. Ostrowidzki

On his thin white wrist there was clasped
A GOLD ROLEX WATCH whose gold plate was
Flaked to reveal a dull undercoat of gunmetal grey. The Fake!
The bastard was a fake: His watches weren't even real gold!

With her eyes gone blue-blacker than
The beads of her grandmother's rosary,
Juanita-Consuella Martinez knew that
If the white cops arrested her, they
Would send her away for a very long time.
So she prayed and she paced. She fretted
And she raved. Then, as if by a Miracle
Of the Holy Virgin-Mother, there was a voice
Which came over her Walkman that told her
In the whip-tongued voice of her grandmother
To RETURN TO THE LAND OF HER ANCESTORS.
Juanita just about freaked when she heard
That. She just about ran out of the room
And gave herself up to the cops without a struggle.
But then she noticed hanging there on the wall
A black velvet painting whose vibrant vista
Vibrated in smoking pastel-blues, blazing
Oranges, smouldering roses, and flaring neon-greens.
Framed in the same cheap chocolate-brown pineboard
Like everything else in the motel-room,
The painting seemed to beckon her
Into a Mayan Temple surrounded by
A lush vegetation of electric emerald;
Though it was only a black velvet painting
Like the kind depicting Spanish villas
With verandas and dusky grape vineyards
Sold to gringo tourists for a slew of pesos
Back on the dusty arid streets of Juarez.

Eric A. Ostrowidzki

Not knowing how she knew what to do,
Juanita literally jumped into the black velvet painting
Depicting the ancient Mayan Temple as if into the
Day-Glo swirling haze of a Whirlpool of Time.
Immediately she was embraced by hot strong winds
And a thousand voices as if she were listening
To a COSMIC SONY WALKMAN which had unlimited channels,
Though she preferred salsa music to the present celestial gabble.
Simultaneous with her entry into the
Psychedelic wind-tunnel of a kaleidoscopic vortex,
Juanita-Conseulla Martinez sprouted a thick fleece
Of tiny rainbow feathers over her entire body
Which helped her to fly through this
Muffled landscape of black velvet rocks and pink polyester
sequoia.
As she approached the beginning of the arrival of whitemen,
Little Juanita of the Lost Barrio near MacArthur Park
Fled that big and bad Conquistador Cortez
And his outlaw band of bandits
Who shot Ticking Golden Arrows
Of envy, murder, cruelty, and greed at her.

With her body a shimmering whorl
Of tiny rainbow-plumage and her long hair
A bouffant mass of kryptonite-green snakes, Juanita
Stood before the sacrificial alter of a Mayan Temple,
Which was a long way from The Tequila Sunrise Motel.
No longer wearing her pink polyester uniform,
Juanita stared defiantly at the coterie
Of Mayan Priests who were just about to
Sacrifice one hundred Brown-Skinned Girls.
In her most polite-to-strangers-voice,
Juanita slammed into the High Priest, "YO, ese,
What you and your gang-bangers
Be doin' messin' with my homegirls like this?

Eric A. Ostrowidzki

You better try burnin' some blue candles
And patchouli oil and smudge stick
Than trying to burn my 'crew.'
You know what I'm saying? You hear what I'm telling you?"
Terrified by this Serpent-Goddess, the Mayan Priests
Decided that times were indeed changing and
Sacrificing a hundred Brown-Skinned Girls was no longer
'politically correct.'
Flying throughout The Empire like a winged rainbow,
Juanita the Serpent-Goddess then persuaded
All the other good brown-skinned people to join
Forces to form a regular whoop-ass Indian posse
Which put to rout many of the Spanish Conquistadors who
Turned into white mules and leapt into the grape-green sea.

Still pissed off about what the Conquistadors
Had done to millions of good brown peoples,
Juanita the Serpent-Goddess ordered
A Great Ark of Gold to be built. After
The Ship of Gold was forged and cast,
Juanita christened the vessel – ROLEX – by smashing
A bottle of California Chablis over its bow; and
Then she ordered the last of the Conquistadors
Who were all on 'social assistance' anyway to be thrown
In golden chains and shipped back home.
By sending the golden ship ROLEX back to Spain,
Juanita turned back Time before her people
Had learned to sacrifice humans and before
The gold-fattened and blood-hungry Spaniards had
Come to steal and rape and murder and torture
And before even the God of Gringos was born.
Then everybody got together and had one bigass
Block party and built a temple of patchouli oil
And blue candles and smudge sticks to the
Rainbow Serpent-Goddess – Juanita-Conseulla Martinez.

Eric A. Ostrowidzki

When Juanita stepped back through the
Black velvet painting like a very hip and very brown
Alice in Wonderland into the drab and dingy
Room of The Tequila Sunrise Motel, she
Still had time to leave before the
Florid portly Little Watch-Salesman came in
And accused her of stealing his GOLD ROLEX
And she killed him by pushing him against
The glass-topped table. She still had time
To change her life before the dirt of whitemen
Would become all that she ever knew. Refusing to
Leave the "House Courtesy Mint" upon the pillow,
Jaunita the Serpent-Goddess began to leave the room,
Listening to Santana's *Black Magic Woman* on her Walkman.
Just as she was about to leave The Tequila Sunrise for good,
The florid portly little Watch-Salesman barged into the room,
Looking all hot and cross and red and sweaty.
Before he got a chance to say or do anything,
Juanita-Conseulla Martinez said in her
Most-polite-to-strangers-voice, "Yo, Caspar, be chill,
Brown-Skinned Girls don't steal Gold Rolexes."
Then she stepped into the roaring orange blast of noonday
And danced across the glittering white asphalt
Of the parking lot,
Full of confidence as if it were the first day of her life.

Richard Van Camp

Twenty Music Videos that Changed My World Forever

Remember that great line in Don Henley's song *Boys of Summer*: "A little voice inside my head said, 'Don't look back, you can never look back'." Well, folks, these are my picks for music videos that, I feel, changed our world forever – especially mine:

1. Michael Jackson – *Thriller* Saw this in Grade Seven as I was training to be a Hockeystick Ninja. When I look back now, it's laughable that I stayed up past midnight just so I could see the "controversial" video, but when I did see it, I was hypnotized by Michael. Even my dad tried doing the Air Walk in his moccasins across the kitchen linoleum. Michael ruled the world for a while – even Fort Smith, NWT.

2. Aha – *Take on Me* Saw this in Grade Nine. By then, I had traded in my nun-chucks for hot knives. Pal Waaktaar's voice is right up there with Morrissey's. Gorgeous video. I actually had tears in my eyes the first time I saw it.

3. Pet Shop Boys – *West End Girls* For one magical summer, Fort Smith intercepted TV's gift to teenagers: "Night Tracks." Night Tracks was nonstop music videos that started at 8 P.M and went until 2 A.M Fridays and Saturdays. I loved it. *West End Girls* is my all time Grade Nine favourite. This video, featuring the pretty boys of pop, showed us a world overseas. Synth driven, beautifully written, stylistically shot. Still one of my favourites.

4. Wham! – *Wake Me Up Before You Go Go* Everything in this video was so bright (!), so happy (!), so fun (!). George Michael's smile was so contagious and his teeth were so white! Suddenly, the world just seemed so happy. When people talk about "The 80's," I immediately think of this video.

5. Peter Gabriel – *Sledgehammer* Peter's videos fascinate me. From alternative excellence with videos like *Shock the Monkey* to *Games without Frontiers,* he graduated to pop video superstar with *Sledgehammer*. After *Sledgehammer*, we expected more from Peter's videos than from any other artist and he came through time and time again.

6. Technotronic – *Pump up the Jam* Saw this video and immediately tried to dance like that skinny black guy who looks like he's dancing for his life. I don't know if the director had a pistol trained on him the whole time and is hollering, "DANCE YOU BASTARD! DANCE!!" but that tune launched the world out of its big hair hard rock frenzy and into an era of techno and dancing like it had never seen before. Suddenly, lyrics weren't everything: the beat was. When you think about it, "When your feet are *stumpin,*'" What the fuck does *stumpin'* mean, anyways?

7. U2 – *With or Without You* Senior High. I finally admitted to myself that music (Thank God) could get me higher than any lame-ass pot. This song was the last waltz on every dance floor on the planet. U2 must have known they had a hit before they left the studio. Gorgeous, gorgeous, gorgeous! Great video. I hated U2 before I saw this video and have admired their work ever since.

8. New Order – *Bizarre Love Triangle* I can't remember who or where I was when I saw it, but the world came crashing down around me when I did. Techno with a conscience. I loved it.

9. Bring the Noise – *Fight The Power* Grade Twelve. My family moved to Calgary for my Grade Twelve year. My brother and I worked at McDonald's and met up with a young lad named Jason Carter. Jason took it upon himself to "educate" us

on what we had missed growing up in the NWT. One of the many bands he got me into was Public Enemy. I hated them at first, but, after a while, with Chuck D's "rhyme animal" instincts, their "get wicked" beat and all that "Yeah boyyy" sniping from Flavor Flave, Public Enemy showed me how angry African Americans were in a new way that informed and educated. I have so much respect for these gentlemen and can't figure out if I'm just plain scared or in awe of Flavor Flave. Great band. Can't wait to see what they'll do next.

10. LL Cool J – *Mama Said Knock You Out* Grade Twelve. Saw this video and wanted to run outside and kick someone in the nuts! Talk about a war anthem. LL Cool J kicked ass in this video – and he was the only man in the ring. Terrifying, what one man can unleash with a song and beat.

11. The Mission – *Wasteland* Grade Twelve. Calgary. In the basement. Black and White concert footage of a band sent from heaven. Had no idea who they were but felt like I had been touched by an angel. I became the first Dogrib goth in history. Hats off, gentlemen!

12. Nirvana – *Smells Like Teen Spirit* When I saw the video, I knew the world was in the way of a huge avalanche of gorgeous noise that we could never walk away from, and we never really did, did we? Kurt Cobain. What a voice. What a loss... I just noticed, however, no one talks about Kurt anymore. What a shame...

13. Madonna – *Bedtime Story* This video finally captured for me what artist/illustrator Dave McKean's dreams must be like. Techno with a spirit. Beautiful but neglected, this video deserves more airplay.

14. <u>Marilyn Manson</u> – *Sweet Dreams (Are Made of This)* Saw this one morning over breakfast in my final year at UVic. I thought someone had rigged up a peep-cam in Hell and was broadcasting footage. "Shocking" is too weak a work to describe this video. Even words like "disturbing" or "raw" fail. Check it out yourself if you need meat for your next nightmare. Brilliant!

15. <u>Tool</u> – *Track #1* More footage from hell. Who are the blue powdered people? What's the story here? Show this to people who never had cable growing up and listen to them age forty years a second while viewing.

16. <u>The Wolfgang Press</u> – *Cut the Tree* This is dark, lovely and mysterious – everything that has ever mattered to me.

17. <u>His Name is Live</u> – *Are We Still Married?* Directed by the Brothers Kozmonov, this video is a strange fable braiding imagery from the nightmares of children. Wow!

18. <u>Metallica</u> – *Until it Sleeps* A Bosch daydream captured on the silver screen. Metallica cut their hair and they look far more dangerous and sharp here. Awesome. Brilliant. Lovely.

19. <u>Sting</u> – *The Angel Gabriel* Haunting. It's like the Devil's circling the last pure angel. The perfect video to snuff that Christmas cheer...

20. <u>Rammstein</u> – *Du Hast* My God. I just walked into someone else's nightmare. Let me get the story line straight. The guy's resurrected through flames by his dangerous buddies while his old lady waits in the car outside the barn and then when he sees her again, after the ritual fire, he doesn't know her anymore. I love it.

I would love to know what your list is...

Richard Van Camp

I Go Bazook!

    (This song's for my Sweet Thang...)

Well I'm shakin' but not weakened
I may be broke, but not beaten
You're my hunnee
My sweetums too
And when I look at you
I go bazook

These mean streets
Don't mean nothin'
This town's talk
Ain't it somethin'?
If they only knew
My love for you
They'd stripp'er down
And go bazook!

Oh she's a lonely road
when you walk it alone
and when you're around
I go bazook.

I'm gonna break the law
I'm gonna have it all
cuz when I look at you
I go bazook!

I'm gonna break the law
I'm gonna have it all
cuz when I look at you
I go bazook!

Oh, I never meant to stray from the heavenly way
But when I look at you
I go bazook!

Yee haw, mama!

Redemption

Kimberly TallBear

A Nomad's Sleep

North American plain, stark in the sun.
The wheat color blinds like snow. Two sisters embrace
under white-breath screams, a hectic sky.
This day, one is leaving.

Closed in the dark rib-cage of a plane,
She shoots over Shannon, Tehran, towards Delhi
to a hastened sunset, sudden morning.
In the nomad's comfort of flight and disorientation,
she sleeps between stars and lights dotting Earth,
seven black miles beneath her. She dreams:

> Running the circle of the dance grounds.
> Dancers come in, gray-haired women, old men.
> Speed past; don't get in their way as they dance
> in like Grand Entry. The circle elongates
> to the size and brightness of Dakota
> fields. Run! Run!
> They are close behind. In mouth, runner's
> spit thickens. Reaching in to pull the sinews out
> like the spider's sticky thread, mouth-water
> beads in black, white, and red
> filling cheeks.
> Spitting handfuls. Can't get all the beads out.
> Can't get out of their way; old people dance slow.
> Run fast! They are close.

In the sky of India, the nomad wakes certain: Flight's in her story.
The story predictably tethers her.

Kimberly TallBear

Strange Gift

Eight Years

Woman, I know your nature.
Four years a silent, big-eyed agent,
I've watched you writhe
in, writhe out.
Spell her, sunder her soul.
My mother, you inhabit
            like a bottle.

Woman, you conjure
men to our manless, midnight silence.
You for a fix forsake us children.
Think too in time you'll trance me
to a cow
to bear your season.

In books, my days, the queen I reign
across those private sovereigns.
But come the apartment
evening, I balance the rope
           or fall

where a net should span,
into the grunt-marked realm
of man. He drives the ground
to rupture – what Mother sole
made level – where she waits
quiescent in red, the hard
day's end.

Kimberly TallBear

Ten Years

Respite for a thousand placid nights
in the reliable creak of bones,
the heat on them, hot medicine mint.
The dark rains a rose.
Grandmother's fingers patter my face.
Rivulets soothe my eyes to close.
Woman, ten years no man's been here
and you slunk away.

The thousandth morning rises.
I wake. I reach
prime for you, five feet.
I wince, I bind, I swathe myself.
Without your body, your bondage gift,
I am plain, yes!
in the old-woman-morning.
Free. I am bloodless.

Twelve Years

Woman, you shadow this river.
You are wanting the wanting boy.
He strokes, an oblivious eel between
the struggle, the current of you pulling me.
Pull me under. Pull through me the brown water.
You burnish my skin, you conjure,
your own soul you summon
              to the bottle.

Like the river, course my body.
Take the boy's hands on me.
I slip between waves to the bank.
I roll out the brown river.

Kimberly TallBear

Water rolls from me like blood.
I stumble under an obscene sun.
Glares me, a messy specimen,
'til I'm hid in the old-woman-house.
Impregnable. My body,
the loot in the dark.

But waiting is
Grandmother. She's resigned
her plum, her mouth.

She's laid them out,
your things to latch and hiss about,
things to catch my body.
She doesn't even hide me.
She urges me into my own bed,
private. Your entrance.
Even she's your apostle servant,
you high priest of
the blood cult.

I wake. I am swollen.
In this bed I am opened.
I could fit the bull or an egg inside.
I lie, mutated.

You try; I will not hunger.
I've seen what whets the addicts
        we become.
Woman, you leave
this girl bloody,
        undone.

Kimberly TallBear

Between Nations

This is the nation of islands
that heaps itself in red
under teeth-bared monuments of war.
It is green with luscious trees
and in the markets where fat rats
drag tails between the crates packed,
across water-worn stones.

Water is heavy, sludges through
like syrup, pulling close
clay-roofed houses, squeezed
and leaning into it.
Soot-fumes of trucks
and hacking motor-bikes lick back
the fat-tongued air.

The transition is not poetic.

In this country are seen
red flags and fists.
I hear of machete stories
and scythes they use among themselves.

I just massacre a language.
Am blind by another nation.
Cannot discern the words
of poets rising
in these pregnant, hothouse islands.

Kimberly TallBear

Anonymity

At the end of the day
when the alphabet letters
and all the history they code
are burned, black symbols, into my sleep,
I would like to slip out of my meat and bones
and waft to the garden, lift my spirit chin to the limes,
temporal-green on emaciated arms of the tree
and breathe earth raised on afternoon rain
and fly up where no human
would ask my country
or name.

Refuge

In yet another new country I am in the cold. By the time the social workers whisk my son & I away from the scummy hotel which holds all of the pensioner's pay checks & breaks all the health rules because the proprietor with the heavy gold chain around his greasy neck pays the health inspector to look the other way. I am considered to be at risk & my last $200 is gone. That was the year of the worst storm in some years, snapping trees like toothpicks. They have met me on a bench at a bus stop 2 blocks away from the hotel & told me not to go back, because I have reported the owner to the public health authorities. I have told them about the lack of clean water, the rats in the kitchen, the dirty mattress in lieu of a crib on the floor & the slop the pensioners are fed at 7 A.M. every morning. The proprietor has already threatened me & they tell me to leave with them immediately and that one of them, who is an ex-marine, will collect my bags from the hotel with far less difficulty than I would.

I travel in the nicely upholstered car with clean windows over a huge bridge, over by-passes and eventually into one of the suburbs and into the refuge where I am given a room. I have 3 months.

Sometime in the afternoon I enter the large main dining room. It is filled with a sea of women's faces, mothers who have on average more than 2 children. There is a palpable strain amongst the people, as though the whole place might blow up any moment. The complex was formerly a hospital. The whole building, with laundries, large washrooms, TV rooms, offices and about 3 floors, is arranged in a square with a courtyard in the middle. I wonder if there is a lot of radiation from the old X-ray section. I have a room in one of the upper wings which hold about 12 bedrooms each.

The first while I speak to no-one, and this surprises no-one, but later it becomes a problem. The women who live there have their own hierarchy, their own order & there are a lot of regular chores to do. No-one talks too much in the beginning. Slowly it becomes clear that I am sitting on a powder keg. These are sexually & physically abused women, women who have been prostitutes, drug smugglers, women who have beaten other women up & who have been beaten frequently in their lives. Many of their children are hyperactive. There is a lot of shouting at meal-times. No physical punishment is tolerated. This does not mean it does not occur. Eventually it is considered that if you say nothing to anyone, you consider yourself superior to others. And that is not allowed.

I have had several talks with the social worker. She says she is not sure I can last 3 months here. She urges me to find a new place immediately because "this is not the place for you." I am oversensitive & I am on the verge of a nervous breakdown. I am trying to come to grips with the idea of violence. I have come from a place, having spent 7 years there, where it is taboo to show emotion, especially any negative feelings. But there are other unspoken things which form the undercurrent of living in this refuge. Staying in my room at all times increases the tension, because I do not mix. I tell her I can't & won't move again until I find a place I can stay in for a long while. I begin to visit women's subsidized rental groups in various suburbs. Always our movements are recorded. We may not be anywhere without it being recorded: precise time of departure and return, so they can buzz me indoors. Regulations do not allow us to be out in the evening without a special pass.

There are almost no books to read. After chores and meals, there is almost nothing to do. There is a lean, wiry-looking woman who fancies herself a budding model, whose long blonde hair fascinates my little son, who tries to run his hands through it as she bends over his stroller. She is a druggie who has the room next to mine, the same chores, and a monster of a little boy who tries to pinch & bite his way through groups of children his age, who screams if he doesn't like someone who is looking at him, as though he has been menaced, which causes his mother to boil up in a rage. One night she is watching TV on the couch beside me in the lounge, something everyone does after 7 P.M. and the child is whining because he wants to move around and she doesn't want him to. She slaps him fully in the face, leaving red marks on it & then he cries for real. None of the women are informers. They talk to each other. They talk to the social workers as little as possible. I am devastated. The only consolation is that my son has not seen this, because he is sleeping in his room. But what I have seen, perhaps, is the reason she begins to become more irritated with me. Because I can get her kicked out.

In the nights I stare at the smoke alarms with their little red lights on the ceilings. My son wakes early in the morning, brilliantly cheerful. I have discovered that I can soft-boil an egg by just sitting it in the pre-heated water from the hot water boxes in the small kitchens at the end of every wing. This becomes part of my routine. Usually no-one comes there, no-one mixes up things for their kids in the morning there, they usually head for the cafeteria instead.

On weekends everyone is locked indoors & security guards are stationed at the gates. For some reason, everyone is more on edge when there is a full moon. They pass the time knitting, playing scrabble or cards and gossiping in a small lounge room at the other end of the wing. Lately I have been hanging in, for about 15 minutes to an hour at a time with the women there. These are mainly Torres Straits women. They are huge, several over 200 pounds. They are the same size as their men, with huge hands that grip the cards. Their plumpness is considered beautiful & they are as strong as water buffaloes. Conversations can run about anything – underwear, sex, fights, jokes. On this night, they have been talking about one of their men, who has threatened that he is coming after his wife that night, security has been doubled & they decide to check me out.

The man has already been spotted moving around the grounds. They have calculated that by coming over the rooftop, the first door the man will come to is mine. Because it is a very likely possibility, one of them asks, "Well, girl, what'll you do if he knocks on your door first?"

"I'll run out the door," I reply.

The room erupts in laughter, long and loud. "What's so funny?" I ask.

"Babe, you are gonna grab anything you can & you are going to try to kill him before he kills you. He's gonna be real pissed off if he doesn't find Sandy & if you leave your kid there, he'll be the first to hit the wall."

Very shortly I return to my room & wait out the night.

Saturday morning, chores before breakfast. Mopping down the floors and cleaning the toilets.

The blonde woman's son is banging on my door again. I can't let him get into where my son is, or sure as hell he'll start trouble. He starts trouble anyway, because I have told him he can't come in, shut the door firmly & locked him out of my room. He has run screaming in rage down the hall.

In a few minutes I have unlocked the door & I am slouching in a chair in the little kitchen outside my room, timing the egg, facing the door. A figure whirls into the room, blonde hair streaming. "What the hell did you do to my son, bitch! Who the fuck do you think you are?"

After that I don't hear what she says anymore. She comes closer, she is screaming & spitting. Night after night I have been thinking about the validity of this "violence begets violence" idea. I am trying to figure out whether it is true or not in all cases, because I'm the only one who can know the answer for myself. This woman is a fighter but I am calculating, calculating . . .

She is younger & quicker. She assumes she can win. I don't have less height, I have less experience, but I have slightly more weight & my mind & my nose feel very, very sharp. She's about 1 metre away & I am watching her eyes.

Time slows down, slows down to one second at a time. She

stands between me & my room, where my son is & if this goes on, he will come for me at the wrong time. And there is only one way to stop her. I am still sitting, my fists have clenched & then suddenly something snaps in my brain. I am no longer, no longer sitting, I have sprung into the air.

In that split second there is a shout from the doorway. Then there are two bodies rolling on the floor and one of them has the other in a headlock and has twisted her arm behind her back. She pulls her up by the scruff of her neck and shoves her out the door, shoves her down the hallway, shouting at her. "You back off! You don't mess with that one," she is shouting. "You mess with her & it is game over for you!"

I'm still standing & then I sit down & I wait until my breathing slows down & the feeling of acidity in my throat & nostrils subsides. "Just missed it," I think & I am relieved more for myself now, than for the other woman. For a moment there, I thought I could have made the wrong decision, but it didn't happen that way.

Within a few days, someone calls from one of the women's subsidized rental groups & I can pack my things & leave – with my answer. As a parting shot, the social worker who had disarmed the woman says, "You were pushing it, but you made it. Take care."

R. Vincent Harris

Souls, Fire, Air, Water, Feathers

The coolness of the fall evening makes our breath freeze into a fog that reminds me of the Grandfathers presence around the fire. The crackling of the fire sends warm blasts of wind in the direction of the four spirits gathered to cleanse and to release the negative energy. Energy that had followed each of the spirits through their lives, destroying their ability to make rational decisions with regards to their purpose on this planet – this is a mission for the Grandfathers. The Grandfathers had assembled the four to guide them in their quest to free the spell of humanness in the mortals. With their spirits broken, the four would, for the first time, see who and what they were to become in their next life. The gathering place was the site of an old industrial school that was once home to hundreds of Aboriginal children and was now a place of good and bad spirits. Here the four would be able to gather among the lost children of the Spirit World.

The fire was hot and the Grandfathers, which are the rocks, were placed in the Sweat Lodge. Water was poured on the glowing Grandfathers and the release of the steam freed the Grandfathers from there sleep, and the flames soared high to the universe in the evening cool air. The spirits looked at one another with suspicion and fear, for each knew that each of the others had an answer that they needed in order to remain in the mortal world. The womb of the mother was a dark shadow in the trees, and as I sat there looking I wondered how many other lost spirits had been in the situation that I found myself in.

It all started months ago when I was on the coast. I woke up with the rippling of waves on my face, and as I woke up I was surrounded by massive black and white fish. Later it would become clear to me that I was a baby whale. I was in a pod of killer whales on our way to the feeding grounds. To this day I never understood why I was brought back as a fish. I had many questions for the Medicine Men who were waiting at the lodge with the Grandfathers. What have I done to deserve this? What lesson was I to take from this? The pod swam all night and I was pushed by mature whales when my body was tired.

Suddenly, the leader shot out in front of the pod. I was so scared that I froze, but was bumped from behind by one of the other whales. As I came up to the surface of the water, I could see a massive steel object moving at a fast speed, with shapes in a variety of colours hanging off the side yelling. I got so scared that I swam under the water to the safety of the pod, and we began to move again.

I started to grow and move faster than the other whales, and I began to swim away on my own, not giving much attention to my family. One day I was out exploring around the rocks, rubbing myself on the pebbles and lying on the surface of the water. The sun felt warm on my shiny black skin, and I fell asleep. The next thing I knew I was in a web of some kind. I thrashed around in the water, but the web grabbed me and I was lifted out of the water. I yelled for my family, but they were too far away to hear. I was in this by myself. I thought, 'what have I done?' I was lowered in a steel tank of warm water. I could barely move around in my tank. The coloured shapes that moved around me were mumbling and making loud noises that sounded like my family. I made the same noise and they yelled and showed their teeth as they looked at me and touched my skin. I blacked out.

When I woke I saw my family. I was happy so I swam fast, but, all of a sudden, I hit a hard piece of water. What I thought was my family turned out to be other whales swimming around in a tank. I was scared and missed my pod. I cried for hours until one of the coloured figures gave me fish, which I ate then fell off to sleep. I had dreams of my family and how I should have listened to the leaders of the pod, to learn from their teaching and to stay close, since they were family and families stick together.

I dreamt for days and what I thought to be another world

was in fact my death from being in captivity. Now I find myself here, surrounded by flames and the other spirits, waiting for the Medicine Man to take us into the womb of the mother, to get a chance at beginning a new life in the mortal world. We gathered around the fire for what seemed for hours, and I asked my fellow lost spirits what brought them here to this point. None of them replied, so I left them alone; after all I should be concerned with my own fate at this point.

We were all ushered into the Sweatlodge to begin the cleansing of the spirits that had brought us here. A loud voice began to sing and pray to the Grandfathers to enter the lodge, to hear our prayers of forgiveness and to ask for strength to not go off the red road again. This red road was our only hope of survival in the mortal world. Once you are off the red road the evil begins and the temptations of the poison of drink, evil smoke the loss of vision of your purpose here on this planet clouds your purpose for being here. Then you are lost until the road becomes clear. This clearing may come after being sick many times. I prayed hard for my past family and friends to keep strong and positive about their life and health, and asked for forgiveness for their wrong doings, and for mine. Then I gave thanks for my experiences in the mammal world and asked for a second chance in the mortal world.

The heat was so intense that I began to see flashing lights in front of me, and I felt my body soar high. I could see the feathers of my majestic wings ruffling in the wind as I looked down on the green fields below. That was when I realized that I was given the body of a bald eagle. I heard the voices of the Grandfathers' saying to me, "Your power, your knowledge, your life, live for the present and teach your lessons of life through the spirit world, and maybe next time you will come to the mortal world and stay."

I did not have any remorse because of my shape that I had been given. I was alone most of the time, I sat and watched over the mountains and the sea, and thought of my past lives and gathered the teachings that I was taught.

One day I was soaring high, and I noticed rippling white waves far below me. I flew in for a closer look. It was the pod of whales. I flew by and let out a screech as if to say hello to my friends. That's when I realized that I was at peace in this life, for I could see that this is where all the lost souls go after they cannot be satisfied on the mortal planet. I was given a life of solitude to fly, to think, to be beautiful, and to be one with myself.

One day I was sitting on my perch high above the river, and off in the distance I could see a form coming closer. I realized it was another eagle. I soared high as if to say, "look at me, I can fly higher than you." I was mesmerized by its beauty. I called for it to come close and land in my tree. Down came the eagle. I was struck by it's beauty, and I realized that it was an old friend who I once knew in the mortal world. We laughed and flew and ate fish for days, and I realized that I wanted him to stay with me forever. So it was that we were together, flying high and being two but as one.

Janet Rogers

Life Beat

Wrapping fleshy covering
Of what was once living
Coat is home to fleas and bugs
Target for hunter's lugs

Working half naked
Wrestling, make it
Warped rawhide
Recoiling, resisting
Tugging, cutting
Satisfying circles

Ground work
Low down
I have found
It best to play
Twisting muscles
Stretching flesh
Lacing lutted openings
Closing into shape

Wind dried
Takes time
Moistened newborn
Taking form
To full grown
Sound

Drummers pound
The heart
They start
It breathing
Drum beating

Sing-ing, sing-ing, sing-ing

Elastic fabric
Animal power in hand
Prayers offered to land
Beautiful
Life beat

Jerry L Gidner

Flute

I sang the wind today
in a mountain field
under cobalt sky.
I sang the wind
sweet and clear,
in a meadow,
boulder-strewn,
where summer's grass was teased
by an ice-blue wind
while the sun shone bright.
I sang the wind with all my soul,
with head upturned and arms thrown wide.
The wind sang me, today,
where lichens grew
and the golden sun
made heath burn red.

I danced today,
with the wind,
my bones a flute
for the earth's soft breath
I spun about
off tufts of grass,
my knees up high,
my heart on fire.
I smelled the world today,
on a hot blue breeze on a hilltop sea.
My life was filled with earth's sweet scent
Atlantic brine and Kansas corn
Buddha's breath and autumn's chill.

Jerry L Gidner

I rode the wind today,
on a clear blue swirl
that touched the sky.
And we looked down,
the hawks and I
on the sloping lea where we once stood.
We gazed down,
at mice below,
whose whiskers twitched
scared to die
I rode the wind,
and it filled my soul,
'til the hawks, the wind,
my soul, the sky
were all there was,
and it but one.

I was the wind today,
singing sweet and singing free.
I was the wind, today,
in a crimson field
where moss was soft
and dead grass swayed
as I danced by.
The wind and I were one today,
in a mountain field,
where granite sighed at our caress.
I became the wind today.
I sang the wind
and it sang me.

Mary Caesar

Northern Sky Dancers

They dance in their spectacular frocks
waving and weaving like dazzling ribbons
streaming in the northern sky.

They frolic gaily
with merry and reckless abandon
as they swoop and crackle playfully
in undulating waves.

They shimmy lavishly with a quiet
boldness and confidence as they
sashay and sway seductively
in shimmering green skirts
dripping with glittering pink tassels.

They are a magical and mysterious
tapestry woven and weaved and revered
in our Native myths and legends
that have been passed on
through the generations.

Sherri L. Mitchell

Sky Woman

Turning my gaze I see her,
suspended in the night sky
swollen and red, eminent,
cycling toward a new beginning.

Blanketed by a sea of stars,
she is cradled in perfect balance.
Delicate Anima, sits stable and glowing,
while her mate shoots wish filled sparks
to fade into the night.

Cradled in a blanket of snow,
I watch them. Understanding then
the harmony of their union.
Internal rhythm is churned,
as calmness replaces chilled trembling.

Exhaling my longing,
to fade into the night,
I feel myself spiraling,
cycling on toward a new beginning.

Amy-Jo Setka

Tea Ceremony

1

I balance on the tight rope
of silences between her words
waiting for answers
Everything is simple
no complications
Everything is sacred
we are busy sipping tea

On the bus ride back
I'll savour the smell of this house
cherish the curling red linoleum
in the little kitchen
I will get down on my knees
scrub the floors before I go
Pine needle soapsuds bruise little corners
of the house that shudders and breathes on its own
This is how we worship
quietly in the kitchen

2

Kohkum regales me with half
of the story as I sit at her feet
The timeworn smell of the little
multicolored rag bags under the table
near her thirty odd six
tempt me with secrets
I know not to ask

This is how I honour her
scrub pots and pans until I can see

my face mirrored, dusting nooks
In Granny's home we sit
tell stories about cousins
I can only imagine what is said about me

I want to take her with me
she must stay and I will always come back
We sit, I bead
Kohkum laughs at my clumsy fingers
stiff from the city. I touch her too much
It can not be helped I need to carry the memory of her skin
that wild look about her I have seen that look in my mother
I have seen that look in me

3

I hug *Kohkum* the last time before I go
bury my face in her neck
Hoping her scent will stay with me for the journey
I caress her gnarled fingers and see my future
in the shape of her bones.

Allison Hedge Coke

Memoir Excerpt

Fish

Come late-season it would begin to rain around three o'clock so often you needn't wear a watch to clock the day. The rains gave excuse for fishing. Sometimes we'd break from the fields and wait just 'til the lightning died down and hurry down to the ponds hoping the rains disturbed the fish in a certain way to make them hit a hoola-popper, beetle spin, or purple worm.

Wiley, the oldest fieldworker in these Carolina tobacco fields, had taken me fishing. We rode over bumpy dirt paths in his red Ford Falcon, kicking up dust and spitting stones along the sides of the fields. We let our tin boat slide into the water and stepped in quietly to fish. The pond was black and stumpy, the sky above gathering clouds, the oar plunking the water with a steadiness, the boat echoing our every move on the still water. A beaver splashing on occasion gave some opportunity to move about in the boat without making too much noise.

We fished all day before I snagged a small-mouth on a yellow devil's toothpick, my favorite top-water lure. He ran the length of my line wrapping two or three times around every stump in the pond, Wiley and I in hot pursuit. We followed the line, unwinding it from the stumps and regaining control of the bass though he never even tried to bite the line, just continued looking for more stumps to wind tying us in terrible knots underwater under the coming storm above and alongside the bank where the mosses grew thick and kept the line heavy at times.

I don't know how we caught him really. Luck maybe, sure, but I think mostly endurance. By the time I got down to just fish at the end of the line (clear of stumps and matter) I knew he was huge. The boat began to pull behind him he had such drag, and Wiley had to hold onto me to allow me to hold the fish. He damn near pulled me in a few times before I pulled him into the boat. Lightning struck one of the trees on a ridge over the bank after we brought in the fish, causing our hair to stand on end, and we got out of the pond as quickly as possible.

We drove the red Falcon down to a bait store halfway up toward town. The shopkeeper laid the bass on a scale and raised it. More than fourteen pounds it was, and I was in my glory. This was the biggest bass I'd ever seen. It was a monster. We went back to the car and began to drive home. I was watching the fish try to breathe in the cooler, gasping, sucking in air, choking on it, yet hanging on. I wanted to stop and roll it in paint to capture its brilliance on butcher paper from the bait store. He was brilliant in beauty and intelligence, well over fourteen pounds, at that weight there was no other way he'd have survived in those waters. Too many predators and too many fishers. I looked over him again and asked Wiley to drive up to the pond just beyond lined-back Hereford cattle pastures. We rolled up over the field stubble and stopped. Rain fell on the windshield and beaded necklaces on windshield stars and down the wipers. Rain fell on the pond in front of us and fish struck through the surface creating more disturbance in waters already alive with pelting. Rain fell over my hands as I held them out the open window, and I told Wiley I intended to let the bass go.

We carried the cooler down to the bank and lifted the fish out, gently holding him against the rain until I lowered him into the water. He lay still. I thought of scaling him with the back of a spoon and slicing his belly to let the guts fall away, and of beheading him. I knew he would be the best-tasting bass I ever ate. I knew it. Every now and then a gill would pump and strain, then Wiley said, "Let's help him." So we pumped the gills in the water, teased each other for our "hand to gill" resuscitation techniques, until the fish caught his breath and pulled away as strong as he had pulled away on the boat and we let go before we even realized he was pulling. He bolted deep beneath the sheet separating this world from the underworld, where creatures who lived long before man ever walked this earth probably still flourished.

Looking at this pond, I remembered early morning fishing and fishing at noon and sneaking out into nearby redneck's ponds and fishing before outrunning buckshot, and finish up by night fishing – jitterbugging – on a cool, calm night, hoping to always be able to live off the water as much as the land. Here, I remembered the cottonmouth that slipped down on my leg in the boat while gigging frogs and how I still had the gig deep in a frog and had to hold the snake out on an oar and to shoot it while it struck toward my shoulder and neck. And how its cottoned mouth glowed in the lamplight and seemed so much the same as field cotton, or cottonwood tufts, seemed so harmless, but bundled between fangs and jaw proved deathly.

I remembered the crack of both barrels in my fury tearing it in half and spraying snake guts in the moonlight from the half-moon on a slow rise after a hot day in the field, moccasins and cotton mouths hanging over our heads from swamp trees growing up out of the water. Snakes which slinked down limbs and into our boats where we'd scramble to gig them and hold them out over the water. And the center or back rider would cut it in half with bird or buckshot from shotguns braced all the while we were in the waters, wedged right between their knees. Snakes four or more feet long, patterned and thick as your arm. Heavy. Snakes with a distinct heaviness which bedded all over these ponds and nested so thick an unknowing swimmer might dive in young and healthy but float to the surface covered with snakes and wholly deceased. We never took a small frog or one singing as we passed by. We always prayed for good days, clear nights, and clean water for healthy kill, for survival.

Now, the immense grandpa of a fish had taken fast under the black water and I realized it was certain I insured the bounty for next year and I recognized and appreciated that mostly we got what we prayed for.

Tracey Kim Jack

Stars for Mary

My close friend, mentor and inspiration, has embarked on her journey to the New World. Mary was an extraordinary friend and elder within our community who shared with me guidance, love and the courage to change. She was a tender loving soul whose gifted deep insight I cherished on each and every visit. I remember how nervous and afraid I felt as I drove myself down her gravel driveway, bunny rabbits hopping out of my way as I parked my car. I was scared. It was well known that Mary was a strong very vocal and often gruff woman who could peer into your eyes and send you running for the bathroom within seconds. Throughout the community she was famous for her blunt and brutally honest nature. Shaking like a leaf, I remember knocking on her door. The time it took her to reach the door and answer seemed an eternity. I looked up at her with my tired watery eyes. Trembling, I revealed my pain, a black chilling cycle sluggishly eating away at my soul.

In retrospect, Mary gently opened her door and welcomed me into her eclectic home. Solid crystals and rocks were everywhere to be seen. I blurted out to her the dark tunnel and the many fears that swirled, whipped and had captured me. As tears streamed across my chapped face, I revealed battered roadmaps scattered like a lost lifeline. I tried to convince her I was not worthy of a new change, that I was not deserving of a new direction, a calmer one. The black years had enlisted many people whom I hurt during my cyclone of pain. Mary cupped her soft, brown hands around mine and with her raven coloured eyes she whispered the truth. She saw past my frightened, blurry eyes and nodded at me to come in.

Through her love, stories and challenges, together with every tear, scream and laughter the dark years disappeared. When we hit that milestone as solid as rock. Our souls danced about the new journey; coiled baskets full of strawberries fresh and renewed. Mary's words were always about those precious berries and to always believe in the power and strength of the universe. It was truly magic how she guided me through that vivid journey, which paved a new way to travel life. Together we celebrated all the gifts the Creator has blessed us with.

During her last summer on this earth she phoned me buzzing with excitement; Mary noticed an ad in the local newspaper. It was a casting call for a feature film to be shot near our little hick town. In a nervous tone (which I rarely saw in her) she quietly asked me if I thought it was worth it for her to try out. Mary thought it would be exciting and something daring!

I gave back to her the same inspiration she had so warmly given to me. I remember my eyes felt bright and twinkly and I giggled with excitement and told her she could do anything! When she got the phone call I felt her heart dancing though the phone. Imagine that, Mary Kruger, Elder from a small REZ with one store and a gas station had landed a speaking role in a feature film. We were overjoyed! That special night we celebrated at our sacred meeting place where a lot of tears, pain and joy were spent. Starbucks!

I remember that night as the crimson sunset painted a violet stream of lines reminding us the hot summer sun had turned in. I can still see that tiny sparkle in her eye, it illuminated the whole Okanagan Valley, brighter than the billions of stars scattered throughout the night sky. From that moment on, we both realized the true meaning of life. To live in the here and now.

What I learned from her I hope to share with the community and the universe. At our darkest time we as women have all faced pain, fear and even sometimes desperation. But we are blessed with very special women in our community that all bear eternal gifts to be shared and passed on. Those gifts are experience, knowledge and silent patience.

I have learned that my bond with Mary is forever and eternal. We can not judge from the past no matter how tempting and convenient that may be. We as women have deep-rooted feelings entrenched in our spiritual connection to our land and our community. We as women offer the backbone and support to all that ask, we all contribute, no matter how big, no matter how small. My prayers are prayers of joy for my dear friend. She may have lived alone in her tiny little eccentric house but she was not alone in the love that surrounded her.

In that sense she was truly blessed.

– February 03, 1999

Theresa G. Norris

David The Bear

There was once a bear named David.

David the bear came from England.

David just loved to play with airplanes. So he moved to another country because there he could play with bigger and better airplanes.

David filled his daily life with the world of airplanes. He found himself a job working with airplanes that flew all over the world! He loved to stand by and make sure that the planes flew on time. In order for the planes to leave on time David made sure that the many passengers, stewardesses, stewards, pilots and co-pilots were safely stuffed into the airplanes. He also saw to it that the airplane's fuel tank was full to satisfaction.

David loved his work!

There was a gnawing problem growing in David's life. When he finished his day working with airplanes, he found, as he sat on his bed waiting for the next day to begin, that he was lonely.

There was nobody in his life that he could tell his stories about airplanes to.

Because David was so busy with his passion for airplanes, he forgot about his social life and he forgot to do his laundry. His bear suits stood in small mountains all over his apartment. It was becoming more and more difficult to get through the door when he came home at night.

One Friday evening he decided it was time to go to the Laundromat.

David filled laundry bag after laundry bag with dirty bear suits. Bear suits for work. Bear suits for play. And delicate bear suits for sleeping in which required special fabric softener. This will take weeks sighed David.

David found the perfect little Laundromat very close to his home. It was even better than he thought because across the street from the Laundromat stood a little English pub and that reminded him of home.

During the day David continued to enjoy his work. And once a week, every Friday, he would wash another bag of laundry.

But he was still lonely.

After fourteen Fridays of washing bear suits David noticed that the mountains in his apartment were growing smaller. He could actually open his door freely, unhampered by a furry pile.

David also noticed familiar faces at the Laundromat.

Slowly at first so as not to frighten people away, David would comment on the freshness of another person's choice of fabric softener. Or he would share little secrets about how much detergent one should use to get the cleanest results for the most soiled bear suits.

Sometimes other bears would respond politely and take his advice. Soon enough some of the familiar faces would share tidbits of their lives.

Weeks turned into months and months turned into years. By now David really looked forward to his Friday nights at the Laundromat. People no longer shared just tidbits of their lives, they shared hefty portions. Not only one bear or two bears but also an entire little group of bears met every Friday night! Between the scent of detergent and fabric softener, hot water and the warm air of the dryers, this cozy little group jabbered continuously. They even enjoyed David's stories about airplanes.

But David noticed something. Even though he still loved his daily life working with airplanes, and he looked forward to every Friday night, he was still lonely.

With closets and chests full of freshly washed laundry, David sat on his bed at night wishing for a friend. A friend he could spend the other six evenings of the week with. Perhaps a friend he could marry. Maybe that friend could even live with him.

David walked through his daily life and smiled at all of the airplanes in front of him.

David observed all of his friends at the Laundromat and smiled as he smelled his fresh laundry.

David walked and walked and walked.

He walked through the city. He walked along its edge.

David was looking for his friend.

David followed all of the signs that would take him to the place where his friend would be.

David was following the signs and dreaming about the scenery around him and not really watching where he was going. To his great surprise he accidentally bumped into Mario. Mario was also a bear, but a little one from a different country.
David toppled over onto the ground and so did Mario. They

both apologized to each other as they helped one another up. David introduced himself to Mario and told Mario how much he loved airplanes. Mario introduced himself and told David that he loved numbers.

They began walking together. David listened intently to Mario's stories about numbers and Mario listened intently to David's stories about airplanes.

As they walked they held each other's hand. David and Mario continued walking together. In the same direction.

That night David sat on the edge of his bed he smiled about his daily job working with airplanes. He smiled about his friends at the Laundromat. And he smiled because he knew that he would no longer be lonely. He had met Mario. Maybe, thought David, we can sit together and count the many airplanes that flew over his house.

And they did.

Carolyn Bereznak Kenny

The Dream and the Vision: Keynote Speech

First Nations Graduation Ceremony
Simon Fraser University, June 5, 2001

Elders, Chiefs, Esteemed Women, Graduates, Student, Family and Friends...

My name in Carolyn Kenny. And my Haida name is *Nang Jaada Sa-ĕdts*, which means Woman with a Mind of High Esteem. My mother is a Choctaw from Mississippi and my father is a first-generation Ukrainian American. I'm adopted into the Haida Nation by Dorothy Bell, of the Eagle Clan. And I hold the crest of the Hummingbird. I'm also an Associate Professor in the Faculty of Education here at Simon Fraser. And my work is in First Nations Education.

It is a great honour for me to have been selected by the graduating class students to offer the keynote address for today's ceremonies.

We are gathering today to celebrate the future.

I say this because the future rests with these wonderful graduates who you see here today.

One of the keynote speakers for a conference a couple of years ago here at the Harbour Centre was Chief Simon Baker, who recently passed away. We were blessed to have such a wise and loving teacher as Si. And he will be greatly missed. Now those precious stories and jokes he shared with us at our conference take on a new significance with his passing. Simon always said "Write it down. That's a good idea. Write it down." He was tremendous advocate for the education of our people. But the beautiful thing about Chief Baker was that he approached everything, including education, with a loving heart – *Khot-La-Cha*, The Man With a Kind Heart.

One hundred years ago another great leader, Louis Riel, said: "For one hundred years our people will sleep. And when they awaken, it will be the artists who lead them."

And of course, now the people have awakened.

Guests, I invite you to look around. Behold the graduating class of 2001. There are the people who will carry us out of our dream and into new life for our people.

The vision. The dream. The dream. The vision.

Visions and dreams are very important concepts for our people and they always have been.

I like Riel's prophecy, his metaphor, his strength, his belief.

We can imagine that our people have been in a kind of sleep. When a people have been colonized, a reasonable choice is to stay alive by being in a dream. How could we have endured residential school? How could we have endured the systematic attempts to dismantle our Indigenous societies through the taking away of our languages, our cultural practices, our singing, our dancing, our feasts, OUR VOICES?? How could we have endured all of this and much more? The dream is a safe space where we can be alive and protect ourselves from such violence.

In a dream, the psyche is very busy. And our people have been very busy in these last years setting the stage for the awakening. Many of our leaders have sacrificed much to make sure that all of the seeds were planted in our dreams, in our society, in preparation for this moment, in preparation for the awakening.

Today, we have in our midst some of those people – the ones who have paved the way. Verna Kirkness, Chief Leonard George...

And of course, we have our strong Elders who have so recently passed to the other side of the veil of life – Chief Simon Baker, Vincent Stogan, Ahab Spence and others.

Policies have been put into place. Embarrassing stories have been revealed, stories of oppression and abuse. The healing has begun. Work has been done to bring our people into the contemporary society in education by holding a drum in one hand and a computer in the other, as Douglas Cardinal has suggested.

The dream is a rich territory. And for a long while, it has been the time to dream.

NOW THE SLEEPER HAS AWAKENED!!

We are getting the education required to sustain our cultures, our values, our beliefs in the modern society. Every year, more and more First Nations people are represented in graduation ceremonies like this one across this Nation. Every year, more and more people are working in our communities to improve the quality of life. Every year, small steps are made toward appropriate research practice, which shows more respect for cultural knowledge.

Sometimes it is very discouraging to be a part of institutional life. Institutions are machines built for efficiency and economy. And they reflect the values and beliefs of the people who designed them – the university, the government, organizations.

It is often difficult for us, the Indigenous people, to find our place in these systems without giving up our own values and beliefs – like love, trust, respect, generosity. These are some of the core values taught to me by my own Native mother. Sometimes we don't see these values reflected in classroom teaching practice at the university. Sometimes we don't see these values in the policies created by the universities, which often advocate a "One Size Fits All" approach. When systems are built for efficiency and economy, the short term view is that it's better to imagine all people as being "the same." This way, the machine can run efficiently and not have to deal with the messy human factor of "difference." And of course, this is why places like the university and the government are so powerful. They exert social control. They advocate a model of the person which suits the mainstream.

How often have you heard bureaucrats or administrators say: "Oh, aren't all people like that? Don't all people value the family. Don't all people believe in those Indigenous values?

Those aren't Indigenous values. Those are generic values."

These dismissive comments, unfortunately, sustain the disbelief of our people that any efforts to "work together as equals" are sincere. These comments are not only dismissive, but they imply the fiduciary attitude which imagines Native peoples as "wards of the state," children, who are incapable of creating their own identities.

But I'm here to tell you that there are allies. There are friends within these institutional structures. These are the human beings who give the institutions meaning. These are the people who are motivated by love, caring individuals with listening ears who are eager to stand beside and even behind Indigenous people – willing to relinquish their "place of privilege" because they know that in the longer view, the visions and dreams of Indigenous peoples will serve us all. These are the people who are intelligent enough to know that in the longer view, it will serve society to deal with the complexities of "difference" immediately, without avoiding the dilemmas that such a critical discourse will inevitably inspire.

AND THESE ARE THE PEOPLE WHO KNOW THAT THE INDIGENOUS PEOPLES ARE UNIQUE. THEY CANNOT BE BOUND BY A PHILOSOPHY OF "ONE SIZE FITS ALL."

Within the graduates you see here today are the beginnings of a new time for our people and for the society-at-large. It is a time "To Reclaim Indigenous Voice and Vision," and a time "To Decolonize our Research Methodologies," a time, as our own conference and now course, here on campus says, to "Revitalize Aboriginal Societies."

And of course, as Louis Riel says, "to awaken."

And what does Riel mean when he says that "It will be the artists who lead them." I can only interpret this powerful statement in my own way. My belief, my feeling, from my own life, my own work, and my own research on the role of the arts in the revitalization of Aboriginal societies, is that it is through the arts of social change. Our pathway to change is vision.

And where do we see the visions and feel the future? In our songs, our dances, our stories. This is our source. This is our connection to Mother Earth. This is the beginning of our way to share our knowledge about education, about social justice, about sustainable ecologies, about ethnobotany, about healing, about many other things.

Wise people are turning to Indigenous peoples who still hold pure and clear traditional knowledge and saying: "Help us to discover what has gone wrong in our environment. Help us to discover what has gone wrong in our governance structures. Help us to find new ways of restoring justice in our societies. Help us to heal."

So, I lift my hands to you, the First Nations graduating class of 2001!!

I lift my hands to you with respect, with love, with trust, with generosity, and say to you the future is yours. The ground has been layed. The dreams have been fed. The visions are waiting. Pass through the door. Lift your eyes to the heavens. And guide us into the future. You have made a commitment to yourselves, to your families, to us, and to all future generations by doing the work of getting your academic education. Now you can add this to the rich cache of cultural knowledge you have had and will continue to have. Now more than ever, you are prepared to CREATE and to share. There are many around you who will continue to support.

But this is your time, your voice, your vision!!

Congratulations!!

Ho'wa

Linda LeGarde Grover

Migwechiwendam

When I look at my grandchildren,
those sweet, happy hearts,
I think with gratitude.

Their bodies are small and light,
and their little feet dance
when they visit
at their grandpa's and grandma's house.
I love their small hands
that bring to me
    a pretty rock
    red heart candy
    a hug
a smile and a sticky kiss.

I am blessed.

Sometimes
I think about my grandmothers.
A long time ago they went to live in heaven,
yet they are at the same time among us.
When I look at my grandchildren
I consider the old days and the present,
today and tomorrow, and the day after tomorrow,
and then I know
that I am blessed, a fortunate woman.

And I think with gratitude.

Migwech, migwech.

Linda LeGarde Grover

Miigwechiwendam

O'o apii ninganawaamabamaag noozhishshenyyag,
      ingiw minawaanigwe'odeg,
nimiigwechniwendam.

Onaangi wii'awensiwaan
      gaye ozide'iwaan naanimiwag
      amanj igo api mawadishiwewaad
      omishomisimiwaa gaye ookomisimiwaa owaakaa'iganiwag.
Ninzaagitoon oninjiwan
      iniw oninjiiniwaan nimbi-biidamawigoog
      wenizhishid asin
      misko'ode ziizibaakwadoonsan
      gikinjigwewin
      zoomiingweniwin gaye bozagozid ojiimewin.

Ninzhaawendaagoz.

Ayaangodinong nimaaminowendam komisag.
Mewinzha giigozi ishpiming
nasaab noongoom megwe'oog niinawin.
O'o apii ninganawaabamaag noozhishenhyag
nimaaminonendaanan gete gizhigoon gaye noongoom,
noongoom gaye waabang gaye awas-waabang,
mii dash ningikwendam
ninzhaawendaagoz ikweyaan, niin.

Mi dash ni miigwechiwendam.

Migwech, migwech.

Linda LeGarde Grover

Redemption

After the Great Flood, *Nanaboozhoo* and four animals floated on a raft looking for an earth surface on which they could live and walk. *Amik* (Beaver), *Ojig* (Fisher), and *Nigiig* (Otter) each exhausted their strengths diving to find where the ground originated, but they were unable to stay underwater long enough to find the bottom. As they despaired, the last and smallest animal, *Wazhashk* (Muskrat), asked to take a turn. *Nanaboozhoo* and the other animals told him that it was hopeless and urged him not to try, but the muskrat insisted on doing what he could. Because of *Wazhashk's* courage and sacrifice the earth was renewed.

Wazhashk, the sky watched this.
Mewinzhaa, long before the memory of mortals,
Wazhashk, the sky watched your timid, gallant warrior body
      deliberate, then plunge
           with odd grace and dreadful fragility
      into translucent black water,
      dark mystery unknown and vast as the night sky
and barely (to a single inhalation shared by a weeping four
and a hopeful splash quieter than an oar) break the surface
into concentric expanding disappearing rings as
water circled your departure,
for a moment transparently covering small soles,
tiny seed pearl toes
above that determined small warrior body
that hurtled from sight then
in an instant was pulled into cold dark depths,
seeking the finite in the veins of a waterlocked earth.

Wazhashk, the water covering the earth watched this.
Mewinzhaa, long before the memory of mortals,
Wazhashk, when you were obscured from the sky

the water watched you
(lost from the sight of the praying four
        alone on a small raft afloat on vast water)
nearly faint under crushing cold
alone then below the waterline
seeking the finite in the veins of a cumbrous earth
as waterfingers intruded and invaded
all unguarded aspects of your small warrior body
now stiff and graceless
pulled by will into icy dark depths.

Wazhashk, in that dark mystery
unknown and vast as the night sky
you continued your solitary plunge
(lost from the sight of all who lived above water,
        who considered your size and your courage)
until in cold and exhaustion your silent voice whispered

ninzegizi nigiikaj
nindayekoz niwiinibaa

I am frightened I am cold
I am tired I must sleep now

and was heard by the Great Spirit.

Wazhashk, you were heard and were answered

   gawiin ni wi maajaa sin
   gaawin gi ga nogan i sinoon

have courage, have courage in the darkness
you are not alone, I am always with you
have courage, have courage in the darkness

til your spirit roused and spoke

I hear, I am here, I will try
through my despair I will

And the Great Spirit watched this and guided you.
Mewinzhaa, long before the memory of mortals,
Wazhashk, the Great Spirit guided you, and watched
your small curled brown fingers
stretch curving black claws
to grasp the muddy, rocky breast
of a waiting Mother Earth.

And today, *Wazhashk*, hear us breathe,
our inhalations and exhalations a continuing song
of courage sacrifice grace redemption a continuing song
since long before the memory of mortals.
With each telling of the story with each singing of the song
we once again rise to break the surface and seek
the finite beyond the grace of this merciful Earth,
the finite beyond the mercy of this graceful Earth.

Horizons:
Voices of Our Youth

Joleen Terbasket

Canoe Trip

I was on a canoe trip
and I heard an Elder say
in the next five years
things won't be the same

If we don't start fighting now, I hear
we'll lose our rights and land
we're sitting here and doing nothing
while precious time is slipping
through our fingers like sand

I heard my friend, Simon, say
Look up in the mountains, the water, the sky
soon this will be a memory
because they will all die

I heard my friend, Trevor, say look at the land
soon it will slowly be taken away
He said, when people don't care, you make them care
even if it's only you who is fighting today.

This canoe trip that started as only a dream
made me feel so good inside
I learned so much I'll never forget
"Good ride for Native Pride"

Joseph Louis

Caged

What have I done
You try to lock me in
I feel nothing but pain
You let me rot inside here
I get bored in here
Let me out
Let me out

All I see is four walls
A hole on one
Its my way out
Locked inside
My head hurts
I think I am going crazy
Let me out
Let me out

Why do you wanna see me like this
I understand my purpose for this
But I will do anything other than this
Just let me out
Let me out
Let me out
I can't take it no more
I hate this place
Please let me out

Johnny-Lee Bonneau

Relate

Chait, Wait, See if they take the bait
Building up my fate, freedom is what I state
Liars is what I hate, life is what I create
To all the Chiefs, hunters and warriors I relate
To all the lands stole, lies told, I debate
Any of the money I make, honeys I shake, I rate
The bro's in prison, the hos envision, to date
In one way to do another it's called Isolate
You also tried to something called assimilate
The dollars in my pocket, the dollars that rocket, I inflate
The white man's taking control of Natives all over the world
Even in New Zealand, they got them sayin' Good day, mate!
But it's this land that you wanted to vacate
So now in this race for the land, better believe we'll take the gate
Years ago there were some Natives that you say you need to investigate
And now one by the name of Mr. Peltier, you incriminate.
Now you want to know my name, ha!
It's too late.

Star Gars

In a galaxy far, far away (the most fashionable galaxy ever)... That's the way star war stories are supposed to begin. So, we didn't want to change the way things are usually done. My name is DavLena and my friend's name is Ratrev. We live in a small town called Trevorland which is close to Hollywood.

Ratrev is four months older than I and she has three brothers. I have six brothers and six sisters. I am right in the middle of them all. Ratrev and I have always gone to school together and we've always dreamed of becoming rich and famous when we grew up. Now we are grown up and we mainly are famous by the locals for our dreaming.

Last year Ratrev and I went to aesthetics school to become nail technicians. We thought we would open our own business in our hometown. Except for the lady named Agnes who lived at the end of town, nobody wanted to have their nails touched.

Life wasn't all that exciting for us in that small town (and we didn't make that much money). One day I finally had enough. I was fed up with the small town and our low profits. Ratrev and I needed to talk.

Since we don't have many customers, we usually do each others nails so we don't lose practice. So while Ratrev was doing my nails I brought up the topic of moving to a city. Ratrev wasn't too excited at first, but after some convincing, she got so excited about the idea she told everyone it was her idea. Anyway, that's how our adventure began.

"Are we almost there yet?" asked Ratrev for about the hundredth time.

"No," I answered a bit sharply, but then decided to say something nice to make up for my sharp words. "But we'll be there in about 20 minutes."

Ratrev turned to stare out the car window again. I could almost feel sorry for her. She's not used to being cooped up for such a long time. Although I must say, a two hour drive isn't that long.

"I know," Ratrev exclaimed interrupting my thoughts. "We could play twenty questions."

"Okay," I said. So I started. "Man or Woman?"

"Man," she answered.

"George Lukas, " I guessed.

"That's not fair," she cried. "How'd you know I was thinking of him?"

"Well actually it was quite simple, considering we are going to meet him!" I ended my statement with an excited, girlish scream. The kind of scream all girls do, which drives my brother crazy.

"I know," sighed Ratrev, "Can you believe that by next week, we'll be doing nails for the most famous Star AC (Armed Conflict) aliens for the next Star AC episode! I've never been so excited in my whole life!"

"Well don't get too excited, there are probably hundreds of nail artists who want to work with Star AC. After all it's only the best movie ever made!"

"I know, but we'll probably be the best nail artists there, after all we've had years of experience and practice in our small hometown."

"Ray," I said using her nickname, "We only went to aesthetics school last year, how much experience could we get in one year, in one town, doing one lady's nails."

"Well," Ratrev paused to think, "When we were kids we always did our friends nails for a nickel. Remember?"

I sat back in exasperation, there's no use fighting with Ratrev. All of a sudden Ratrev cried out, "Look!" she exclaimed "Hollywood!"

We decided to go to our hotel to freshen up and to get a bite to eat before going to the studio. We found the hotel, no problem. It was right next to the studio, so that was plus. We had a shower and changed into some fresh clothes then headed to the nears hamburger eatery. We had heard from Agnes that

McDannie's was excellent for a quick meal. I had a Big Mc and fries that were in the shape of cows. Ratrev had a famous McDannie milkshake and chicken chunks. After dinner we headed down to the studio to meet the producer, Nick McKullum. He was a nice guy, he showed us around and introduced us to our nail rivals. after a quick introduction we got started. Nick gave us each some nail polish and a rubber hand so he could analyze our skill level. We had a secret ingredient for extra speedy drying of the nail polish and one short cut to nail sculpting. The we had to do a written test to show our love for Star AC and our creativity and our knowledge of nails. It was so easy. I had a gut feeling we'd win. Ratrev thought so too.

"That was so easy!" she exclaimed while we were leaving the exam room. "I just know we'll win!"

"And just how do you know that?" I inquired.

Ratrev looked down in embarrassment, "On top of the extra speedy drying nail polish and the short cut to nail sculpting, I might've left Mr. McKullum some cookies with our exam paper."

"You did what?" I couldn't believe it, but that was Ratrev, and there was no changing her.

The next day we had breakfast in the hotel and went to the studio to see the exam results. I was so nervous. I wanted to win with all my heart. If we didn't win we'd have to go back to Trevorland and everyone would think us fools for trying something so crazy and insane.

"You know what?" Ratrev said, breaking into my nervous thoughts.

"What?" I asked.

"I feel sorry for all these people."

"What?" I asked again, somewhat confused.

She looked at me as if I were crazy. "You know, all the people who will have to go home because they lost the contest."

In spite of my nervous feeling I had to smile at Ratrev's confidence. I walked into the exam room with a renewed confidence maybe we would get the job after all.

Once we were all seated Nick McKullum came in and we quieted.

"Welcome back." he said. "I'd like to thank you all for coming back and for applying for the job. The exams were very well done and..."

I couldn't listen. I just knew we wouldn't make it, maybe I should leave to save myself the embarrassment. I was just about to get up and go when Nick said something that made me faint.

"The winners that will be working on Star AC are DavLena and Ratrev!"

I awoke to see Ratrev's excited face looking down on me.

"We did it!" she said excitedly and she seized me up into a big bear hug.

I had never been so excited or embarrassed. Everyone was looking at me, I was lying on the ground, apparently I had fallen with a half sigh half scream, which came out as a very odd sound indeed. But who cared, we won. We'd get to meet all the Star AC actors and actresses and all the makers of the films and George Lukas! This had to be the best day of my life.

And it was the best day of my life. Even to this day I still remember it like it was yesterday. The work was so fun. I got to meet all the movie stars. It was so fun doing the nails. I did normal nails for the people and for the aliens, I got to do talons, fun shapes like spirals, and cool designs. After we finished that episode, Nick asked us to stay on for the next one, so we did. We were extra thrilled because Georgie and the rest of Star AC were to film in our very hometown, Trevorland. This brought a lot of excitement to Trevorland and brought extra income to the locals.

When we finished all that, other producers found us and we got more jobs. We travelled around and had so much fun, but we never forgot Trevorland and our dear friend Agnes. We went home to visit as often as possible.

We made a goal and achieved it. Now because of our special talent we are thinking of opening up a nail technician shop in Hollywood.

Ratrev asked, "DavLena, what would be a good name for our shop?"

We decided to call it Star Gars. We would do special tasks for special effects movies. And that's our story, our adventure. So long and may aliens, spaceships and nails be in your dreams.

Shawn Wildcat

Untitled

He wears honour and pride in
this scarred mask. Shaking visions from
his hair, echoes of vast dreams. His
dance flowing with spirits and sweetgrass.
Speaking ages.
As the night breeze progresses, eyes fade.
But before he fades, he moves into the fire
. . . and we are cured.

Shannon Wildcat

Generations

We often look toward the future
and seldom the past.
Hoping our ancestors' memories will last and last
Books and pictures will come and go
for our future we will not know.

Shannon Wildcat

Looking Back

Now as you grow and see the world,
You will often forget why you must respect your Elders.
Think far back to a time of:
Teepees,
Moccasins,
and Traditional hunting.
Remember your grandfathers telling you stories,
of all the hard times
of being used for techniques, beliefs and land.
Your ancestors once spoke in a language,
some of you will never know.
They have experienced more than you could ever bear.
There was a time when land,
was shared amongst us all.
Now there is no trust passing.
Trust, respect, believe in yourself.

You have the spirit of your ancestors in you.

Biographies

Biographies

Rachel Bach was born in Calgary, Alberta. She is originally from Columbia Lake which is in the Eastern Kootenay area. She has a strong Ktunaxa/Kinbasket ancestral background and history. She is a 14 year old 'A' student in Grade Ten. Recently Rachel received excellent marks for her term paper on Aboriginal Self-Government. Rachel has a great interest in reading.

Mariel Belanger is a member of the Okanagan Nation and a mother of three. In 1995 Mariel's 17 year old brother was killed in a tragic car accident. After that time, many of her poems reflect feelings in relation to that tragedy. Mariel is presently pursuing an acting career in film and television and has now fulfilled her dream to become published.

Donald Blais identifies as Métis (of Penobscot heritage). He divides his time as an instructor of Aboriginal spirituality in the Department for the Study of Religion at University of Toronto, a part-time youth development director, and as an author in various genres.

Johnny Lee Bonneau is an 18 year old from the Okanagan and Nlaka'pamux Nations. He is currently in Grade Twelve and plans on travelling to Thailand after graduation. Johnny is an accomplished athlete in fastball and hockey.

Shirley Brozzo is Keweenaw Bay Anishnaabe from Marquette, Michigan. She is currently employed at Northern Michigan University (NMU) where she coordinates a retention program for all students of colour on campus. She is also an adjunct instructor with the Native American Studies Department. Shirley has earned a BS in Business Administration and a MA in English writing, both at NMU. She has had over twenty-five poems and short stories published. Shirley also has three adult children, Jamie, Brandi and Steven.

Mary Caeser is a Kaska Dene from the Liard First Nations from Watson Lake, in the Yukon Territory. She is an artist, a writer and a mother of two sons. Mary attends Malaspina University-College. Her goal is to complete her diploma and obtain a Fine Arts Degree from the Emily Carr Institute of Art and Design in Vancouver, BC.

Biographies

Karen Coody Cooper is an enrolled member of the Cherokee Nation of Oklahoma. A writer and finger weaver, she has worked in the museum field for more than twenty years. She obtained a Masters' in Liberal Studies from the University of Oklahoma and works at the Smithsonian Institute in Washington, DC.

Janet Duncan is a Gitksan woman, and resides in the Nicola Valley with her young family. She works full-time at Nicola Valley Institute of Technology as a bookstore coordinator and library technician. Janet has a two-year certificate in territory management, and plans to finish the Native Indian Teacher Education Program and become a teacher. She loves to write poetry, songs and short stories.

Jack Forbes is a professor of Native American Studies at the University of California at Davis. He is of Pawhatan/Renápe, Delaware/Lenápe ancestry. He received his Ph.D from the University of Southern California. Forbes was born at Bahia de los Alamitos in Suanga (Long Beach) California. Professor Forbes has served as a Visiting Fulbright Professor at the University of Warwick, England, as the Tinbergen Chair at the Erasmus University of Rotterdam, as a Visiting Scholar at the Institute of Social Anthropology of Oxford University, and as a visiting Professor in Literature at the University of Essex, England. His latest book *Red Blood* is published by Theytus Books.

Gordon M. de Frane is of Chemainus and Penelakut ancestry. His play *Drawing Down the Moon* was workshopped at the Crazy Horse Aboriginal Playwrights Festival. At the First Peoples Symposium, in 2001, Gordon presented a paper on the subject of Chosen People, also known as Two-Spirit People. Gordon is a storyteller, and has told stories for the elementary school system in Victoria, and read at many poetry readings. He is in fourth year undergraduate degree in Humanities, English, and Writing Major. His goal is to graduate. He plans to be a storyteller for future generations of Aboriginal Peoples.

William George is from the Tsleil-Waututh Nation in North Vancouver. He is published in various anthologies and literary magazines. Publications include: "Mountain Bedded Rock", "Sockeye

Salmon Dream" and "My Pledge" in *Gatherings*, "Movement Will Pass" in *A Shade of Spring: New Native Writers* by Seventh Generation Books and "Blanket Need" in *Let The Drum Be Your Heart*, edited by Joel Maki and published by Douglas & McIntyre.

Jerry L. Gidner is a member of the Sault Ste. Marie Tribe of Chippewa Indians and a life-long environmentalist. He currently works for the environmental program at the Bureau of Indian Affairs in Washington, DC, and has been an environmental educator for a county parks department and an enforcement attorney for the Environmental Protection Agency. His wife and daughter provide the daily poetry to his life.

Linda LeGarde Grover is a member of the Bois Forte Band of the Minnesota Chippewa Tribe. She teaches in the Education and American Indian Studies departments at the University of Minnesota, Duluth, and has published poetry in *The Roaring Muse*, *The Eclectic Literary Forum*, and in several anthologies, including Native Women in the Arts' publication *My Home As I Remember*. Her poetic themes often include aspects of her research on government Indian boarding schools and the effects of government policies on the lives of Native children, families and communities.

Heather Harris is a Cree-Métis poet, artist, traditional dancer, professor and mother living in Prince George, BC. She teaches in the First Nations Studies Program at the University of Northern British Columbia and is nearing completion of a Ph.D.

R. Vincent Harris is a member of the Sioux Valley Dakota Nation. His first play *Touch* was produced at Brandon University and at the Crazy Horse Aboriginal Playwrights Festival. In 2001 he participated in the Summer Institute of Indigenous Humanities at Brandon University. Vincent lives where his writing and spirit takes him. He is currently a student at the En'owkin International School of Writing, Indigenous Fine Arts Program at the En'owkin Center in Penticton, BC.

Biographies

Allison Adelle Hedge Coke is mixed Huron and Tsa la gi. She has a MFAW and has done Post-Grad Work at Vermont College; and the Institute of American Indian Arts. Currently she provides teaching residencies for the South Dakota Arts Council's Artist-in-the-Schools Program, South Dakotans for the Arts' Corr Program in juvenile facilities, South Dakota Humanities Council Scholars Lecture Program and performs as a Touring Artist for the South Dakota Arts Council.

Tracey Kim Jack is a freelance broadcast journalist and producer for television news and documentaries. She is a member of the Okanagan Nation, born and raised on the Penticton Indian Reserve. She received grants from the Canada Council for the Arts and the First Peoples Cultural Foundation to produce documentaries and film screenplays. Her educational background is from the British Columbia Institute of Technology and Media Arts Program at Capilano College through a scholarship from the Chief Dan George Memorial Foundation.

Debby Keeper was born in Calgary, Alberta. Keeper is a member of the Fisher River First Nation, a Cree community located in the Manitoba Interlake region. She received a Bachelor of Fine Arts General Degree Honors from the University of Manitoba in 1996. Keeper is a multidisciplinary/multimedia artist who has been active in the arts community since 1986. Her educational and artistic background includes: media arts (video, audio, computer arts); visual arts (painting, printmaking, photography, drawing, collage, ceramics, graphic design); performance (theatre, voice, vocalist); and writing (poetry, essays). She currently lives and works in Winnipeg, Manitoba.

Carolyn Kenny (Nang Jaada Sa-ĕts) is an associate professor in the Faculty of Education at Simon Fraser University. She supervises the Indigenous Peoples' Teacher Education program and the Indigenous Peoples' Master of Education program. She also serves as senior supervisor for Indigenous students in doctoral programs at SFU. For twenty-five years she worked as a music therapist using an approach based on her Aboriginal values. Her ancestral background is Choctaw and Ukrainian. She is adopted into the Haida Nation as the daughter of Dorothy Bell, Eagle Clan, Hummingbird crest. She has one daughter, one son and one granddaughter.

Bradlee LaRocque is Dakota/Anishnaabe. He is a Saskatoon based artist whose genres include photography, sculpture, performance and new media. His work was included in the 1996 exhibition *Native Love*, which toured across Canada. LaRocque is a founding member of Tribe (Aboriginal Artist Centre). Since 1986, he has been extensively involved and has played a significant role in social and cultural movements concerning Aboriginal rights and social issues.

Joseph Louis is a 17 year old from the Okanagan and Secwepemc Nations. He is currently in Grade Twelve and plans to attend college after graduating.

Charles L. Mack is an enrolled member of the Rosebud Sioux Tribe. The Rosebud Sioux Reservation has been his home most of his life. He is currently working at the Rosebud Sioux Tribe Office of Water Resources. He has attended part time for the past two years at Sinte Gleska University. His goal is to someday write a fiction or science-fiction novel.

Annie Rose Major is from the Nlakapamux Nation in the Nicola Valley. She speaks and understands her own language. She has two beautiful children, Brenda Lee Major and Bruce Lyle Major. She is blessed with one grandchild, Mckayla Annie Gracie Nelson. She has also gained another son, her son-in-law Steve Nelson. She is currently attending the Institute of Indigenous Government in Vancouver, BC. Her future goals are to succeed in the field of Associate of Arts and Science in the Institute.

Rasunah Marsden is of Anishnaabe and French heritage and born in Brandon, Manitoba. She received a Bachelor of Arts in English Literature from the Simon Fraser University. She also completed teacher certification and course work for a Masters' in Fine Arts in Creative Writing at the University of British Columbia. She currently teaches Creative Writing at the En'owkin International School of Writing in Penticton, BC.

Biographies

Sherri L. Mitchell is a Penobscot Tribal member, from Bur nur wurb skek, Penobscot Indian Reservation in Old Town, Maine. A Program Director of NACHME, Native Youth Leadership & Community Building Program, Sherri facilitates Native Youth Leadership and Substance Abuse Prevention programs. She is currently working on her first book, which discusses the social, mental, emotional and spiritual needs of our children.

MariJo Moore, Cherokee, is the author of *Spirit Voices of Bones, Crow Quotes, Tree Quotes, Desert Quotes, Red Woman With Backward Eyes and Other Stories*, and editor of *Feeding The Ancient Fires: A Collection of Writings by North Carolina American Indians*. She was chosen as one of the top five American Indian writers by Native Peoples Arts & Lifeways Magazine. She serves on the Board of the North Carolina Humanities Council and the National Caucus for the Wordcraft Circle of Native Writers and Storytellers.

Leah Morgan lives in Calgary, Alberta, but is originally from Kitwanga, BC. She also has strong ties to the Nuu-chah-nulth territory on Vancouver Island. Her interests are to build strong and healthy communities and continue on with her goals of educating herself.

Daniel David Moses is a Delaware, born at Ohsweken on the Six Nations lands in Southern Ontario, Canada. He holds an Honors B. A. in General Fine Arts from York University and an M. F. A in Creative Writing from the University of British Columbia. He lives in Toronto where he writes full time and is associated with Native Earth Performing Arts. His plays include *Coyote City* (a nominee for the 1991 Governor General's Literary Award for Drama), *Big Buck City* and *The Indian Medicine Shows* (both Exile Editions), which won the 1996 James Buller Memorial Award for Excellence in Aboriginal Theatre.

Duane Niatum is an enrolled member of the Klallams (Jamestown Band of Washington State). He was born and lives in Seattle, Washington. Several of his essays on contemporary American Indian Literature and Art have been published in magazines and books. His seven published works include, *The Crooked Beak of Love*, and soon to be published *The Pull of the Green Kite*. He is presently teaching in the department of English at Western Washington University.

Theresa G. Norris was born in Edmonton, Alberta in 1957. In 1989, Theresa moved to Amsterdam in the Netherlands, where she now lives and works running her own small business. After a long journey both physically and spiritually she has gained the gift of perspective on her Cree family and heritage.

Sandra A. Olsen has been writing poetry for over ten years; although she has only recently come forward publicly with her work. She has won three Poetry In Motion contests. As well, she has participated in various stage performances including BC Festival of the Arts/Indigenous Arts Service Organization.

Karen W. Olson is Cree/Anishnaabe from the Peguis First Nation in Manitoba. A single parent to Krista Rose, this former CBC Radio journalist is writing stories that bring reality and tradition together. No longer inclined to 'hold back the bad parts' or 'hide the spiritual side' Olson is taking risks that challenge an internalized fear of saying too much. To renew their energies today, the Victoria based author and her daughter take part in a women's fast each spring on Peguis.

Eric Ostrowidzki belongs to the Odanak Band of the Abenaki Nation in Quebec. He is a single parent of two boys, Gabriel and Jeremy. Eric received his Bachelor's of Arts and Masters' of Arts in English literature at McGill University, as well as his Diploma in Education. Eric worked as an ABE English instructor for the University College of the Caribou, for the Alexis Creek Band within the Chilcotin territory. He works as an Assistant Professor, teaching English at the Institute of Indigenous Government. Recently he has completed and submitted his dissertation for his Ph.D in English Literature.

Frances A. Pawis (Anishnaabe) in 1997 reached one of her dreams and graduated from the Aboriginal Teacher Education Program at Queen's University. She studied to become a teacher so she could encourage and motivate children to believe in themselves and to love

Biographies

learning. Many poems were written while in her studies. She says children are wonderful and they inspire and motivate her.

Brent Peacock-Cohen is a member of the Lower Similkameen Indian Band, which is part of the Okanagan Nation. He is enrolled at University of BC working towards a M.Ed. in the History of Education. He received a BA from the University of Victoria in History. He has also received an Associate and Certificate in Mass Media, Public Relations and Journalism from Kwantlen College-University.

Janet Marie Rogers is a visual artist, writer and playwright of Mohawk/Tuscarora ancestry from the Six Nations Territory in Southern Ontario. Janet has seven self published chapbooks of poetry she has created under the name Savage Publishing and two books of poems published by Fine Words Chapbooks in Victoria, BC, where Janet has been a resident since 1994. Her artwork graces the pages of her book entitled *Mixed Meditations (of an Urban Indian)* and her photographs are included in her latest book, *Sun Dance, Poems from the Red Road*. In the summer of 2000, while at the Gibraltar Point Centre of the Arts on Toronto Island, Ontario, Janet created a play which features Mohawk poetess E. Pauline Johnson and legendary painter Emily Carr.

Cathy Ruiz is of Métis-Cree background and has been writing poetry since age 13. She has shared her work with a variety of audiences in print and on stage including with the Seattle Poetry Festival, National Public Radio, Raven Chronicles, and two poetry anthologies. She is currently working toward a Master's degree in the Humanities and teaches creative writing to adults and children.

Margaret McKay-Sinclair Ruiz was born in Grand Rapids, Manitoba in 1919 and is Métis-Cree, Scottish, and French. She immigrated to the United States in 1948. She worked most of her life as an assistant buyer in department stores until she retired fifteen years ago. She has always loved literature and has been taking writing classes for seniors for about seven years. Last year she completed a book of memoirs.

Biographies

April Severin was an invited reader at Eden Mills Writers Festival 2000. April is the author of three chapbooks *Testimony*, *Witness* and April's most recent title *Atatawi* (Gift) is deeply rooted in North American Native spirituality and celebrates the Earth's gifts, and addresses environmental issues. Her publishing credits also include nature poetry in six consecutive editions of *Tower* (the biannual publication of the Tower Poetry Society).

Amy-Jo Setka is Métis. She is a Graduate of the En'owkin International School of Writing and Fine Arts.

Kimberly TallBear is Dakota/Arapaho and a member of the Cheyenne and Arapaho Tribes of Oklahoma. She earned degrees from the Massachusetts Institute of Technology and the University of Massachusetts at Boston. She is a founder of OyateDuta, a research and planning organization headquartered on the Sisseton-Wahpeton Sioux Tribe Reservation in South Dakota. Her research is focused in two areas: race and tribal governance and how contemporary Native American and Indigenous poetry reflects or challenges restrictive notions of Native authenticity. She has published poems in numerous journals around the world.

Joleen Terbasket is 14 years old and from the Lower Smilkameen Indian Band. She is in Grade Nine at Smilkameen Secondary School.

Richard Van Camp was born and raised in Fort Smith, NWT, and is a member of the Dogrib Nation. He is the author of *The Lesser Blessed*, which was recently translated into German by Ravensburger. He has two children's books out: *A Man Called Raven* and *What's the Most Beautiful Thing You Know About Horses?* illustrated by George Littlechild. He has a collection of short stories out with Kegedonce Press titled *Angel Wing Splash Pattern* and is currently attending University of BC taking his Master's Degree in Creative Writing.

Barbara Vibbert is an Odawa with the Wikwemikong Band on Manitoulin Island, Ontario. She was born and raised in New Brunswick, and has lived and worked throughout Canada and the United States. Barbara is a retired city planner/project manager, liv-

Biographies

ing with her husband of 40 years. Previously her poetry and short stories have not been published and have been shared only with family and friends until now.

Bernelda Wheeler began broadcasting at the age of seventeen and had her first writing published. She refers to herself as a communication artist because her work has taken her into acting in all media, public speaking, conducting writing workshops and public information work. Items have been published and broadcast in local, regional, national and international outlets and take the forms of script-writing, columns, children's books, poetry, and short stories, among many others. As a child, she thought books were magic – writing even more so.

Shannon Wildcat is 16 years old and currently in Grade Eleven. Shannon takes a big part in her school drama department and hopes to pursue a career in this area. Shannon is part of the Ermineskin Band in Hobbema Alberta. Poetry is a big part of Shannon's life, it helps to express the way she feels and what she's thinking.

Shawn Wildcat is 19 years old and is of the Cree and Okanagan Nations. He is currently preparing for college. "My writing is of a world that is not necessarily of this one, I use ojects from this place as symbols for a deeper meaning. That's the logical way to explain it, but to me, it's just the way I see things."

Connie Crop Eared Wolf is the 47 year old mother of André, Jill, Alanna. She and her husband Andy hail from the Blood Reserve in Southern Alberta. A high school teacher by profession, 2001 is her debut as a Doctoral student at the University of Calgary. She holds her Master's Degree in Education; a Bachelor's Degree in Education and a Bachelor's of Arts Degree. Writing poetry is a recently discovered talent of hers.

Candy Zazulak is descended from Manitoba Swampy Cree and Seauteux Anishnaabe ancestors mixed with Scottish and Welsh. She was born in the Purcell Mountain Range at Kimberley in the southeast corner of British Columbia. Her childhood was spent in

Biographies

Winnipeg, teenage years in Ontario and adult years in Vancouver. Candy received her Associate of Arts Degree from the Institute of Indigenous Government in 2000.

AGMV Marquis
MEMBER OF SCABRINI MEDIA
Quebec, Canada
2001